# REDCROSSE

## THE STORY OF
## ST. GEORGE AND THE DRAGON

Young Readers Quorum

Redcrosse:
The Story of St. George and the Dragon

Frank P. Araujo

Young Readers Quorum Sacramento, CA
Contact: YoungReadersQuorum@gmail.com

Cover design and artwork by Pine Dysart-Bricken.
Interior design by M. Anne Sweet.

Copyright © 2021 Frank P. Araujo
ISBN 978-1-7372178-0-0
Revised Edition: October 2021

Young Readers Quorum

# REDCROSSE

## THE STORY OF
## ST. GEORGE AND THE DRAGON

**Frank P. Araujo**

**Illustrated by**

**Pine Dysart-Bricken**

Young Readers Quorum

This folktale is based in part on the lay of The Redcrosse Knight, from Canto I of the first book of *The Faerie Queene*, by Edmund Spenser. However, this story does not embrace the symbolism or political views of the original and is a work of fiction derived from the St. George legend in its various forms and sources.

In Memoriam:
Mary Agnes Juncker Araujo
(July 2, 1944 – May 7, 2021)

*Sansloy charged without returning the salute.*

# 1.

# HECATOMB

## The North Country

FROM BEHIND THE MOUNTAINS, dawn in a blaze of early morning sun-fire melted the shadows around the small houses scattered around the farm fields. Sounds of roosters crowing blended with the mooing and bleating of the farm animals rending the morning air.

A huge shadow burst through into the eastern sunlight. The flying figure emitted a piercing cry, echoing throughout the rolling hills, bouncing off the mountains, resounding among ruddy hillsides. The fields became pockmarked with dark burning splotches that fouled the fresh morning air with the odor of sulfur.

Red-sparked flashes popped among the small houses. Jagged flares marred the dawn's light.

Planted fields, trees, and houses erupted into flames. Smoke boiled, roiled up in black columns forming into dark clouds. The shadow surged through the smoky overcast. Streams of flame shot from the dim figure striking houses below. Thatched roofs lit up in scarlet bursts. Villagers quickly pulled open their curtains to see jagged flares marring the dawn's light. The shadowy figure surged through the smoky overcast shooting streams of flame. Thatched roofs, planted fields, and trees erupted into flames. Smoke boiled up in black columns, forming dark clouds.

"The Dragon!"

Flecks of sparks and ash filled the reddish air. Villagers streamed out from their burning houses, threw snatched-up possessions into wagons, grabbed children. Sulfur and acrid smoke stung their noses and eyes while they scrambled, shoved, some on foot, others pulling wagons and pushed to join in a line along the main road. The faces of the men and women showed terror, their children cried in fear. Lugging their scant possessions, they scurried through smoke-filled shadows into the light of the new day.

A woman asked her husband, "Where'll we go?"

He strained, pushing against his wagon's yoke, his face disfigured like one fleeing a pack of wolves. "I know not," he muttered.

At the head of his mounted guard, Brenin Wylle spurred his horse over the rise in the road. He reined to a sliding halt, stood in the stirrups, and scanned the scene below him. His gray eyes pulled into a squint, he watched his subjects fleeing their burning homes. He shouted above the noise of running feet, squeaking wagons, and the crackle of burning fields, "People of the North Country, return to your homes! We will protect you!"

The people grumbled. Many cried. Most just hurried on ahead.

At the Brenin's side, Arglwydd Larn, Captain of Guards, rubbed his scarred face. His dark eyes probed those of the man wearing the crown in front of him. "Shall we stop them, Majesty?"

Brenin Wylle sank back into the saddle and said, "Let them go."

The horsemen turned back toward the city.

"Majesty." Larn reined up next to the Brenin. "What's next?"

"We wait, Larn."

"Let me and the men lay an ambush ..."

"We've already lost too many good men," the Brenin said.

Larn moved in closer. "I worry about Princess Una, Majesty."

"I know. She's hard-headed."

"She might go to the Cave of Winds—that business with the peasants' children."

"I forbade her," the Brenin snapped. He stopped, shook his head. "She's like her late mother. She'll do what she wants."

*****

On the road out of the city, the cart bounced over chuckholes and bumps. Princess Una gripped the sideboard, eyebrows knit, eyes fixed on the road in front.

"Can't we go any faster, Gyles?" she said.

Gyles's leather cap clung to his head flapping like an old hound's ears. He slapped the reins and shouted, "Get!" at the team of horses.

"This is not safe, Highness," he said.

"We've got to get there before they do something foolish."

"Who, Highness?"

"Those people."

"Yes, Highness. People can be fools."

Una steadied herself on the bumping seat. "I've heard rumors, Gyles."

"Rumors?"

"Of a man telling the people that human sacrifice will appease the beast."

Gyles flinched, gripping the reins. "I know nothing of that, Highness."

"Who'd say such things?" Una said.

Una scowled and pointed up the slope at a bend in the mountain road.

"Oh, no!" she cried. "They've already been there. Hurry, Gyles!"

When Gyles pulled up near the mouth of the Cave of Winds, Una jumped down and ran toward the opening in the side of the mountain.

Coming to the flat, sandy landing in front of the cave, she halted, stunned at the litter of charred bones. She coughed from the hanging sulfur smell and, picking her way through the carnage, she stopped short. A burnt rag doll—arm gone, dress blackened, lay in front of her. She picked it up.

"We're too late!" she said.

She squeezed the tiny doll in her fist, her eyes smarting from the smoke and sulfur.

"Damned hell beast!" she screamed. "I'll see you dead! Hear me?"

She staggered back to the cart and climbed in. Gyles slapped the reins on the anxious horses and they burst into movement.

"To the palace, Highness?"

"Yes."

Without words, she held the singed doll tight until her knuckles turned white.

"They're great fools, Highness," Gyles said.

"Yes."

The cart bumped over the rough road. Jolted from side to side without caring or noticing, Una sat up, her fist still clenching around the doll.

"I will go to Troynouvaux."

"When, Highness?"

"Tonight." She sat up, back straight, lips clenched. "I'll get help from the Faerie Queene."

\*\*\*\*\*

## Troynouvaux

Uther in the light green tabard over his chain mail looked over at the tall man beside him wearing a white tabard with no colors or markings on his armament or white helmet as they walked into the tourney lists.

"Barstair is wily," Uther said. "Don't let your guard down."

"I won't," the man in white said, his voice muffled through the face guard.

"Keep your attack in front. He's been squire to Sir Kylan; he's seen every trick."

"I hear, Uther." The white helmet twisted; blue eyes staring through the eye slits.

Uther looked around. He said, "Many remain."

The white helmet bobbed. "Her Majesty too."

Uther slapped the arm of the man in white. "Concentrate on Barstair."

White strode to the center of the list where Barstair, a shorter man dressed in dark blue with a falcon's head design on his chest cover, stood alone in the field of combat. White squared swords and shields with Barstair, turned toward the royal box, and both men dropped to one knee.

Three heralds gave blasts on trumpets. The Faerie Queene Gloriana rose to her feet. Slender body. Angular face. Two wire-like buds poking up from her hairline, wasp-thin wings extending behind her shoulders. Fixing her dark eyes on the two combatants in front of her, she said, "Senior Adjutants. Do your best."

The two men faced each other with weapons raised. The crowd cheered, and the horns fell silent. The men circled each other like dogs.

Barstair began a series of three feints and false attacks, his movements ferret-like. He crouched to offset the reach advantage of the taller man. With a shout, Barstair swung the double-edged sword in a head cut, then turned at the last moment in a cut to White's shoulder.

White took the blow on the edge of the bulky tourney shield and whipped back a lightning riposte to Barstair's arm. The blow drew blood. The crowd roared. Barstair shook the pain off and crouched deeper.

They fought. The heat of the dying day bore on them. They fought. Both were spotted with bloody cuts and marks. They fought. Their breathing came in grunts and pants. They fought. Each man probed for an advantage, tried to draw the other to expose a weakness, shook the ache from weary arms and blinked from the sting of sweat in eyes. And they fought.

In the great chair of her royal box, Queene Gloriana watched with the intensity of an owl tracking two rats, dark eyes never wavering from the two combatants.

"They fight well, Majesty," her attendant Lady Tyreena whispered.

"Yes," Gloriana said. "Much depends on this little war."

"What is that?"

"Much." Gloriana's tone was final. Tyreena leaned back.

On the field, White stood his ground as Barstair feinted and dodged. In a quick movement, White swung at Barstair's head. His shield came up. White's blade fell short and curved in a short arc, striking Barstair's side. White followed with a series of four head cuts. Barstair closed in to block White's swing short. Barstair thrust, then ripped up, catching the edge of White's shield. He jerked on the shield, snatching it from White's arm. White cried out, gripped his sword with both hands, attacked again and again. The Barstair fell back, raising his shield against the onslaught. White hacked to the edge of Barstair's shield, knocking it from his grasp.

White pressed the attack. Barstair made a head cut while he was falling back, and he stumbled. White pushed forward, crashed into him, and swept his feet from under him. Barstair fell. White knocked his sword from his hand with one sweeping cut.

"Sword!" Barstair's hoarse voice rang across the list as he rolled away. "Allow me to retrieve my sword."

There were cries of "No! No!" White stepped back. Barstair rose to his knee. White lowered his sword. Barstair lunged, tackled White, drew his poniard, and held it to White's throat.

"Yield." Barstair's voice rang out.


Queene Gloriana was on her feet, a little smile playing across her face. She raised her hand and cried, "Put up, Sirs."

Both men came to their feet, stepped forward, and knelt on one knee in front of her.

"Well, Adjutant Barstair," she said, "you fought with guile."

Barstair tore off the dark blue helmet. His dark hair and

dark eyebrows glistened with beads of sweat. His broad face broke into a grin.

"I didn't actually yield, Majesty."

"So, I see. You win the match but lose the day."

The grin vanished. His dark eyebrows wrinkled.

"Majesty?" he said.

"Oh, you'll be knighted soon enough." Gloriana turned to the man in white, his head still lowered. "Remove your helmet, Adjutant."

He removed the white helmet, his blond hair, and brows over blue eyes wet, his face spotted with dirt. He kept his head lowered.

"You will make the vigil tonight," Queene Gloriana said. "Tomorrow, you will be dubbed and known in my service as The Redcrosse Knight."

# 2.

# TROYNOUVAUX

## The Palace Courtyard

NOW WEARING A VEIL, Una pushed through a crowd of vendors, travelers, and entertainers outside the palace. Turning to the dwarf following close behind her, she said,

"Wait for me here, Arnax."

People stepped to one side making scowls, side glances, and mumbled protests. The sentry at the gate blocked her way with his halberd.

"I've come for an audience with the Queene," Una said. "Please let me pass."

"Everyone wants to see Her Majesty!" the sentry said.

"I'm Princess Una, daughter of Brenin Wylle of the North Country. I've not come to bother Her Majesty with trifles."

"Corporal of the Guard," the sentry called out, "A royal visitor without."

The unsmiling corporal stepped forward.

"A royal visitor!" he said. "Well, I suppose we'd better admit her."

Una followed the corporal into the inner courtyard over protests from the throng outside the gate.

"Hoi! I've been here for two days!"

"Who's she?"

"Not fair!"

Upon entering a room in the courtyard, the corporal pointed to a quill, ink, and parchment on a table.

"Write your business and fix your name to it."

Una sat, wrote, and took a ring from the purse hung around her waist.

"Have you wax?" she said.

The corporal sucked in his breath. "No, Mistress."

Una licked her finger, smeared some dust from the table, rubbed it on the parchment and pressed the ring into the smudge. The corporal took the parchment and bowed.

"Please follow me where you can wait in comfort, Mistress," he said. "I'll present this to the Royal Chamberlain."

The Chamberlain came into the hall where Una waited. The filmy wraps of her gown flowed out behind her, as delicate as her wasp-like wings. Her voice had the quality of a high-pitched bell, "Princess Una of the North Country?"

"I am."

"You are most welcome. I'm Her Majesty's Chamberlain, Minatrix. What is this urgent business?"

"I'm instructed to relay this matter directly to Her Majesty."

"By whom?"

"By my father, Brenin Wylle of the North Country."

The Chamberlain reread the parchment, brushing her

finger over the imprint of the ring on the dirty smudge. She motioned with her hand and said, "Come this way, Your Highness."

They walked down two long mirrored halls into an anteroom filled with the buzzing of Troynouvaux citizens. In a low voice Minatrix said, "These folk seek audience with the Queene."

Scratching their bulbous noses, trolls shook dirty, shaggy beards.

Elves darted glances with bright eyes, touched the tools in their belts.

Merchants waved their arms and argued with each other.

Diplomats posed, spoke among themselves and used broad gestures.

Forest gnomes hunkered on the floor in silence—all turned, staring at Una and the tall Faerie passing through their midst.

Arriving at the end of the corridor, at a nod from Minatrix, two hawk-faced guards swung open the massive doors. Una followed Minatrix into the huge chamber. Bangles, bobbins, cut glass, and crystal hung suspended from the ceiling by the thinnest of webs scattering beams and sparkles of light everywhere. Glimmers and glints moved across the walls causing Una to blink at the continuous wash of changing colors.

Dazzled, Una said, "This is like falling into a rainbow."

"Quite," Minatrix replied.

Una went on, "Or stars."

"Or stars indeed."

At the end of the room the empty throne stood near an open window. At its massive foot, a great Siberian tiger stretched out flicking the end of its tail. Two peacocks perched, cackling on the windowsill. Two more tall hawk-faced guards stood at the inner doors of the throne room. Small groups of people talked in hushed voices.

A pair of Faeries—one in bright cinnabar gossamer, the other in lush purple—whispered in the chirruping tones of their language.

Diplomats dressed in their traditional garb regarded Una with hostile curiosity.

A pair of wild Saxon thanes stared at her from bearded faces.

Ladies of court whispered behind their fans.

Minatrix and Una strode across the floor over signs of the zodiac engraved in tiled mosaic. Motioning Una to stop at the throne's raised dais, Minatrix said, "A moment, Highness."

Minatrix then disappeared into a curtained chamber behind the throne.

Una looked around—the walls of the great chamber caught her eye. They were etched with colorful pastoral scenes of nymphs and fauns, dancing to pan pipes, watched by deer and forest animals. The blue ceiling, painted with frescoes of the sun, moon, and stars, arched overhead. The entire room sparkled, bathed in refracted light from the dangling prisms. Minatrix reappeared and said, "Her Majesty grants you audience."

A tall man, the Queene's Beadle, showing a mottled red face, bright red cloak, and cap, stepped out of the chamber, and strutted to the center in front of the dais. He struck the floor with his long staff.

"He reminds me of our rooster," Una said.

"Oyez, Oyez, Oyez, Citizens, guests, friends of Troynouvaux. Her Majesty, Queene Gloriana, the Faerie Queene."

The two hawk-faced guards drew back the curtain on both sides. Una dropped into a deep curtsy.

The Queene was tall like Minatrix. Her proud face bore a warm smile. She wore the same filmy gown as the other Faeries with a thin gold crown around her brow; the light reflected off her gown in multicolored flashes. Her dark eyes missed nothing as she sat on the throne. Minatrix chimed, "Majesty. Princess Una from the North Country."

The Queene motioned to approach.

"Majesty, I'm Una, daughter of Brenin Wylle of the North Country. For some time now, a dragon has terrorized our kingdom. We ask your help."

"Tell Us of this dragon."

"It lays the countryside to waste and destruction. It terrifies our farmers. They sacrifice their livestock to it to appease the great beast. But the monster still rampages and destroys. Farming has all but stopped. Our tenants run away daily. We're very nearly impoverished."

"Why haven't you destroyed this creature?"

"We've no army. Most of my father's knights are gone

now, most slain by the dragon—others have simply fled. Only my father's personal guards remain."

"And the people?"

"The people run or hide in helpless terror."

Una paused and took the singed, broken doll from her side purse. A diplomat gasped. Una went on, "We've learned someone has told the farm folk that if they sacrifice their children, it will placate this horror. Some have even foolishly tried it."

"Enough said!" the Queene said. "We'll send someone to dispatch this evil."

Princess Una's eyes filled with tears. "We pray for a party of noble champions."

The Queene whispered to an attendant who went behind the curtain. Several minutes later, she returned with a young man. He was tall, blond, blue-eyed and wore a suit of mail covered with a white tabard that showed a bright red cross. His tabard and armor were new—he wore no sword. The Queene said, "The Redcrosse Knight will take up arms for your cause."

"Your Majesty. Forgive me for observing, he's but one and noticeably young at that. Surely, you've someone more experienced."

"We select the Redcrosse Knight."

"Majesty, this dragon has killed my father's best knights. You must realize the …"

"We do not take your request lightly, Princess Una. As We said, the Redcrosse Knight will champion your cause."

*The Queene said, "The Redcrosse Knight*

*will take up arms for your cause."*

"Majesty, this is a great beast! We've been forced to live in a brass tower!"

"Princess Una. You've made known that which your kingdom requires. We've no doubts Redcrosse will attend these needs."

Una lowered her eyes before the gaze.

"Very well," she said. "When can we leave?"

"This very eve. I shall speak to the Redcrosse Knight first."

Una curtsied and strode to the great doors. When the two sentries swung them open, she paused and glanced back at the Queene and the young knight.

# 3.

# REDCROSSE

## The Throne Room

THE QUEENE WAVED HER HAND and the court withdrew. Turning to Redcrosse, she said, "We charge you to go to Princess Una's kingdom in the North Country and dispatch the cause of evil and mischief there. When you complete this task, return here to our service."

"Majesty, the Princess has little confidence in me," Redcrosse said. "I too have doubts."

"Listen to your doubts, Redcrosse. They will keep you cautious."

"I've never been on a quest."

"After today, you'll never have to say that again."

"It would be a lie of omission if I didn't admit my lack of experience."

"Noted. We know these things."

Redcrosse looked up into Queene Gloriana's eyes.

"I will do my best," he said.

At the Queene's signal, a servant brought up a battered shield. Repainted white, it bore the same red cross that Redcrosse wore on his tunic.

"Take this shield with you," the Queene said. "It has a name, *Amddiffyn.*"

Redcrosse took the shield, hoisted it. "This shield is old but has a just heft."

"You'll be armed and provisioned for the journey. Use it well."

Carrying the shield back to the men's quarters, Redcrosse paused, hearing a familiar voice call out to him. He looked up to see his mentor, Sir Allyne, the list master.

"It's off fighting you'll go," he said. "I hear too you've a very lovely charge."

"I am given a quest."

"I hear it's a dragon."

"It is."

"Frightened?"

"I am, truly."

"It's courage to admit to the stench of fear, lad," Sir Allyne said. "Only liars or fools deny it. Few have ever faced a dragon. Fewer still have lived to tell of it."

"It's not the fear of death that makes me ache."

"What then?"

"All men die. I fear failing."

"I've taught you all the fighting skills I possess. Time alone hones the keen edge that makes a warrior. Never forget—great warriors are those that survive."

"Am I good enough for this task?"

Sir Allyne slapped Redcrosse's shoulder. "Self-doubt is a

curse of youth. Remember: a knight can lose his sword arm and still fight with the other. But you've only one head. Use it well."

"I will."

"One thing more, lad."

"Yes?"

Allyne unbuckled his sword belt and clapped it around the young knight. Redcrosse protested, "No, Sir Allyne. Not your sword!"

"Lad, the sword, *Arety*, has served me well all these years. The blade was forged by trolls—it can slice stone and keep its edge. Never draw it unjustly and once drawn, never sheathe it without honor."

"I swear, Sir Allyne."

"Fight the good fight, Redcrosse."

Sir Allyne embraced the young man, walked away without looking back.

Upstairs in the men's quarters, Redcrosse stuffed his personal possessions into a leather bag and looked around at the place that had been home for most of his life. After a moment, he picked up the shield and stepped out to make his way down the stairs to the armory below.

When Redcrosse arrived at the armory, the old armorer said,

"Ah, Sir Redcrosse. Told me you'd be here."

"I need gear, tack ..."

"I know, I know. 'Tis all here."

The old man hobbled over to a pile of gear. Redcrosse looked over the equipment. "Where's the helmet?"

The armorer handed Redcrosse a helmet. Flat steel straps curved across the white crown, the red top straps matched the red cross on his tabard and shield. The face piece had a single horizontal eye-slit with steel pins meshed over the eye slots for protection. The old man said, "Here 'tis, Sir Knight. This helmet will turn sword, mace, spear, or anything else."

Redcrosse wrapped a binding cloth around his head and the armorer slipped the helmet over it. The helmet fit well, the wide, mesh-covered eye-slit allowed a wide field of vision.

"It's comfortable," he said.

"Amazing fit, Sir Knight. Wear it in good stead."

Shouldering his equipment, Redcrosse crossed the court to the smithy. The one-eyed armorer looked up when he came in.

"Your sword!" he said "Sir Allyne's *Arety*. None finer. And the Welsh shield, too! Wait here."

Taking a key from a hook, the smith hobbled to the back of the room, moved things aside to reveal a tall case. Unlocking it, he took out a long-bladed lance with a black handle. The old smith held out the weapon with both hands to Redcrosse.

"The *necator draconis*, the dragon slayer," he said. "The blade was forged from steel smelted from iron that fell from a star. The handle and haft are fire-hardened, crafted from the single root of a blackthorn tree."

Redcrosse wheeled the smooth handled spear. "It falls well in the hand."

"It's been kept under lock and key all my life. Now, by order of Her Majesty, it's delivered to you."

Stepping out into the back courtyard, Redcrosse made his way to the stable. He called in to the head groom, "Thobus, I'm here for a mount."

A tall man with a long, face led out a large gelding, its mane and forelock a dark black, his steel-gray coat a myriad of black flecks and ticks.

"Your mount, Sir Knight," Thobus said.

The big horse with bright, alert eyes nuzzled Redcrosse's cheek with the whiskers around its muzzle. Redcrosse patted the horse's neck. Thobus, impressed with horse's choices, nodded approval.

"He likes you, Sir Knight," he said.

"You chose well, Thobus."

"I chose not, Sir Knight."

"Then who?"

"Her Majesty."

Not known for long explanations, Thobus saddled the horse and handed the young knight the reins. "Thobus, has the horse a name?" Redcrosse asked.

"Telum, Sir Knight."

"Telum?"

"Because he's as fast a flying dart."

Redcrosse led Telum out of the stable to the mounting

block. He was about to step up when he heard a bell-like voice. "Redcrosse."

Minatrix was standing at his elbow. He started to drop to one knee.

"None of that," she said. "I've known you and that Welsh scamp since you were boys."

"Thank you for coming, My Lady."

"Stand on the block, Redcrosse."

Redcrosse stood on the mounting block and the tall Faerie fit a pair of silver spurs on his heels.

"These will keep your behind on horseback," she said. "At least I'll know you're properly fitted with good spurs."

Redcrosse mounted Telum and turned to the door of the courtyard. Before he passed through, a tall figure stepped out of the shadows into his path.

"You'd leave without a goodbye?" the man said.

"Uther!"

Dismounting and gripping his friend's hands, Redcrosse said, "I'm told to attend immediately."

"Understood. We wish you well, but not without a bit of envy."

"Good friends."

"I hear it's a dragon."

"It is."

"Afraid?"

"I am."

Slapping Redcrosse's arm, Uther said,

"At least be a bit arrogant so no one'll notice."

They laughed. Redcrosse looked over at the saddled horse and said, "I must go."

"I've something for you."

Uther took a medallion from his neck and slipped the chain over Redcrosse's head. The medallion was gold and cut with a dragon's head within a fiery circle.

Redcrosse looked at the design in the fading light.

"What's this?" he asked,

"My family crest. Wear it."

"But, it's yours, Uther."

"It's now yours. It marks you as my brother and will bring you luck."

Uther stepped to the horse's left side, bent over, and formed a cup with his laced fingers, Redcrosse placed his knee in Uther's hands, threw his leg over the horse's back, and put his feet in the stirrups. Uther stood back and raised his hand in salute.

"Go, Redcrosse. Fight the good fight!"

Redcrosse rode Telum out of the courtyard, into the world beyond.

# 4.

# DEPARTURE

## Beyond the City

REDCROSSE, ASTRIDE TELUM, rode alongside Princess Una who rode her white donkey. Arnax the dwarf followed behind, his short legs moving in a rapid trot. The road from Troynouvaux twisted through rolling farmlands, spotted green hills, and brown villages.

The day wore on. Una did not speak. From time to time, Redcrosse glanced over at her. She ignored him, keeping her gaze straight ahead. Looking toward the setting sun Redcrosse said, "Highness, we'll pass the night here."

"Very well."

Redcrosse tethered the mounts and let them graze. Arnax gathered kindling and firewood. They ate without conversation. Redcrosse stepped out alone to survey the area. Returning, he saw Una asleep by the fire and covered her with his cape before he lay down and fell asleep to the sound of the crickets.

The next day on their travels, the landscape changed to flat farmlands and they picked up their pace. Una spoke in a curt voice, "Thank you for the cover last night."

"It was nothing, Highness."

At midday, they stopped to water their mounts and drink at a spring. Una asked, "How long have you been in Queene Gloriana's service?"

"I was dubbed knight last month."

"After some battle?"

"No, I was in a tourney."

"Did you win some honor?"

"No. My opponent lost his sword and I let him recover it. I turned my back and he fell on me with his knife. It was his match, but Her Majesty called me into service."

"Why, if you lost the match?"

"It was her will."

Una said nothing more.

They made camp that night at the foot of a mountain surrounded by forest. Howling from the woods made their mounts skittish. His eyes wide, Arnax rose to his feet.

"Wolves!" he said.

"Wolves are only fierce in winter," Redcrosse said. "They'll not come near our campfire."

That night, the howling came closer. Redcrosse awoke to see Arnax and Una huddled close to the fire. He got up, took his sling from the saddle bag, picked up a rock, and hurled it into the woods. A yelp, some growling and snarling, and then the patter of retreat sounded through the underbrush.

"They're not really bad fellows," Redcrosse said. "Those old tales about wolves have little truth to them."

Una snorted and huddled down by the fire while Arnax sat

staring at the embers. Redcrosse unsheathed his sword and walked into the bushes; stars twinkled in the night sky over the mountain. Redcrosse paused to listen to the night sounds before he returned.

"They've gone, Arnax," he said. "Get some sleep."

"Thank you."

In a few moments, the little man was snoring.


The next day they crossed from farmlands into rolling hills. Coming through a little valley between two mountains, they entered a dense forest. Sunlight turned to shadows in the foliage of the trees. Una and Arnax huddled close to the knight.

They heard no bird or animal sounds. As they went deeper into the forest the mounts became nervous. Redcrosse brought the shield to his hand and loosened the sword in its scabbard. Dense brush grew thick among the trees and the twisted road made a sharp bend.

A loud, screeching sound erupted, and a large animal leapt out of the dense undergrowth and sprang at Una. The donkey shied, almost throwing her. Redcrosse spurred Telum and threw up his shield in front of her. The talons of the monster ripped across the metal surface.

"Dear God!" Una cried out. "What's that?"

"Gryphon!" Redcrosse shouted. "Back into the woods!"

Arnax seized the bridle of Una's donkey and pulled her back into the safety of the trees.

The gryphon was the size of a lion, with leathery wings

*"Gryphon!" Redcrosse shouted. "Back into the woods!"*

and eagle-like talons on its front legs. It had the head of a raptor, the eyes of a viper, and it hissed, showing its sharp, hooked beak, when it lit on the ground.

Clapping on his helmet, Redcrosse faced the gryphon, shield up and sword drawn. The creature moved from side to side, lashing its serpentine tail, looking for an opening. It crouched as if ready to spring, launched by its powerful leonine rear legs. Telum moved in, keeping his head toward the gryphon. The creature arched its pointed tail, armed with a poisonous sting, and leapt onto the neck of the horse.

Redcrosse jammed the shield to stop the thrust of the gryphon's tail into the horse. Greenish yellow venom spattered over the white of the shield. The horse gave a piercing whinny of pain as the creature dug its talons into his side and snapped at his neck with its beak.

Redcrosse struck and severed the gryphon's head from its body. The body fell, twitched a few times, and lay still. Arnax peered from behind a tree, still holding the bridle of Una's donkey.

"Is it safe?" he said.

Redcrosse sheathed his sword.

"It's over," he replied.

Arnax led Una's donkey past what remained of the gryphon. Coming to a nearby stream, Redcrosse washed the foul-smelling venom from his shield. Hearing a noise, he looked up to see a man in a monk's habit scurrying toward them. He was tall and bearded with wide, staring eyes, his mouth in a broad smile. He stopped and stared at Una.

"I heard the noise of a battle," he said.

"It was brief," Redcrosse said. "The gryphon's dead."

"Great joy!" the monk said. "You've rid the woods of that evil creature."

"Who are you, Father?" Una asked.

"Father Daniel. I've lived in these woods for years. Come, dine with us."

"We will," Una replied.

The monk led them to a cottage on the edge of the woods. A large monk met them; his face hidden in his cowl. He poured wine and prepared food.

Father Daniel indicated the monk in the cowl, "My acolyte, Brother Typhon keeps a vow of silence."

"May he be blessed," Una said.

"Come drink, Sir Knight," Father Daniel cried out. "To a most noble victory."

He leered at Una. "How lucky to have such a brave fellow attending you, lovely lady."

Una declined the offered wine.

Redcrosse sat down and took a swallow. Father Daniel kept talking, his wide eyes getting even wider.

Redcrosse felt tired. His head spun and he began to feel sleepy. He closed his eyes—the gryphon was back. It sprang at him. He raised his shield, struck with his sword. The gryphon was too strong; his sword bounced off its reptilian hide. His arms were weak, and his sword felt heavy. The gryphon's face was just in front of him ... the sting on the tail waved, menacing ...

"Sire, Sire. Wake up!"

The voice came as if out of a fog. Redcrosse struggled to open his eyes.

Cold water drenched him. Redcrosse shook his head like

a dog and stared at the dwarf before him, who was holding a bucket in his hand.

"The monks!" Arnax cried out. "They seized Princess Una when you dozed off."

Redcrosse stumbled to his feet, grabbed his sword, and ran after the dwarf into the woods. They pushed through brush and scrub until they came to a cave in the side of a hill.

"They took her in there!" Arnax said.

Sword drawn, Redcrosse charged into the cave. Ignoring an explosion of hundreds of bats, he plunged into the dark. He called out, "Princess Una!"

Redcrosse heard a muffled voice and moved toward it. Spotting a dim glow of light, he felt his way in its direction. The passage opened into a chamber of the cave. A candle flickered on top of a barrel. Una sat on a rock, gagged, her hands tied behind her. Redcrosse tore the gag from her mouth.

"They were not monks!" she yelled. "He was a sorcerer, said his name was Archimago. They fled when they heard you coming."

Redcrosse cut her bonds.

"You're safe, Highness," he said.

"Well, safe enough for now!"

Redcrosse led her out of the cave into the fading sunlight.

"You should watch what you drink, Sir Knight!" she snapped,

"I will, My Lady."

"I'm not Your Lady."

"My apologies, Highness."

Una composed herself as Arnax led them back to the cottage. She changed her tone and said, "I forgot my manners. Thank you for rescuing me from those evil men."

"And from the gryphon," Arnax added.

Una spoke between clenched teeth, "And from the gryphon."

"What matters is our quest," Redcrosse replied. "I'm sorry for these delays."

They went back and found their mounts. Redcrosse helped himself and Una to the food.

"Is it safe?" she asked.

"Oh yes, Your Highness," Arnax said. "I had some just before I heard your cry and woke up Sir Redcrosse."

They entered the moors beyond the woods and made camp off the road between two hills. That night Redcrosse slept little and awoke several times. He whispered into the night, "Archimago! Who are you?"

# 5.
# RENEGADES

### Near a Village

BEYOND THE MOORS, Redcrosse, Una, and Arnax came to some farmlands surrounding a small village nestled just off the road near a stream.

"We can stop and rest there," Redcrosse said.

Una nodded agreement and they picked up the pace. Before they reached the village, a farmer with a scythe on his shoulder stepped out of a wheat field. He doffed his cap and bowed.

"Hail, Sire and Dame," he said.

"Good day, fellow," Redcrosse replied. "Can we rest and take refreshment in this village?"

"You can, but be careful. There be bad men about."

Loosening his sword in its scabbard, Redcrosse asked, "What bad men?"

"A band of brigands," the farmer said. "They wander in, take what they want, leave and never pay."

"That's thievery," Redcrosse said. "I'll not permit any of Her Majesty's subjects to suffer such tripe."

Una interrupted, "Remember—we've a quest."

"I can't ignore innocent people putting up with a band of renegades," Redcrosse answered. "Especially the poor."

"Just keep your attention on the task at hand," Una said.

"Thank you for reminding me, Lady."

The farmer led them to the village.

"Mind, Sires," he said. "There's no inn, but for mere coppers, the Widow Kearns sets well a table."

"How many in this band?" Redcrosse asked.

"Twice four, Sir Knight. But too, there's Burcell. Big fellow with leathered armor. He's chief rogue."

"Are they armed?"

"Well, they've cudgels, knives—one a mace, another a boar spear, Burcell a sword. Ah, there's one—the one-eyed rogue—has a bow."

"Perhaps we shouldn't stay here, Princess Una," Redcrosse said.

"On no account!"

"But for your safety, Mistress," Arnax said.

Una glared at both of them.

"I intend to eat a cooked meal and wash my feet," she said.

"Your mistress is going to the village, Arnax," Redcrosse said.

"They may be gone," the farmer said. "Them knaves alight and flit like rooks looking for some morsel."

Coming into the village, the farmer showed them to the Widow Kearns's house. The widow marshaled her sons to set a large table under a tree. She brought out roast meat, cooked vegetables, and bread.

After they had eaten, Redcrosse went to tend their mounts. Una called for water and, while the village girls watched, washed and dried her feet. Una smiled and called them over. They flocked around her, touching her hair and clothes, asking questions all at once. A voice called out,

"Whatta' we got here? 'Tis a little nun."

"Yea, a nun," another said.

Una turned to see four men on scrawny horses. She flinched at the smell of the heavy body sweat of the men and horses. The speaker's face was black with dirt and grime; his eyes shone like a weasel's. A second man with a dilapidated leather helmet leered at her over his bulbous nose. The third man's dirty blond hair spiked out like a cocklebur. The fourth man's greasy leather cap gave drooping ears to his rat-like face.

Showing yellow-green teeth, Dirty-Face said, "Well, little nun, how's about some of God's blessing for us today."

"Watch your tongue, you foul-smelling churl," Una snapped. "I don't tolerate insults."

The four men broke into loud laughter. Three more men rode up. One sported a dirty, stringy beard tied in a knot under his chin. Another was tall, bald, and thin as a rail. The last one was a dirty-faced boy of about fifteen. They all rode without saddles on the same scrawny horses as their mates.

Dirty-Face slipped off the back of his horse.

"I think the nun should give us a little kiss," he said.

"Stand!"

Redcrosse rode up on Telum with sword drawn.

Dirty-Face stopped in his tracks.

"What do you do here?" he said.

"Get on those flea-plagued nags and feel the wind on your backs down the road."

The men moved back. The thin, bald man said, "We've no quarrel with you."

Redcrosse advanced. "I have one with you. Now ride on."

Dirty-Face scowled.

"We didn't know the nun was yours," he said.

"Leave or fight!" Redcrosse said.

"Hold, Knight!" a new voice called out. "You've no call to order my men around."

A large, jowled man in worn, ill-fitting, leather armor with a rusty sword in his belt came up. He sat in an old saddle on a horse little better than those of his band and positioned himself to Redcrosse's left.

Redcrosse did not move. He said, "Then you'll answer for their poor conduct."

"If the lads've offended, then, I apologize. I'm Sir Burcell, Knight of the Realm."

"What realm?" Redcrosse asked. Burcell smiled, waved his arm across his chest.

"Why, that of our good Queene Gloriana of the Faerie folk," he said.

Redcrosse moved Telum in front of Una. He said in a low voice, "Get in the house."

Una retreated behind the rump of the big gray into the cottage. Turning to his fellows, Burcell said, "Ah, that's nice. The little nun has gone behind her knight."

Movement from behind Burcell's horse caught Redcrosse's eye. He raised his shield and spurred Telum; an arrow clattered off his shield. Redcrosse drove the big horse into Burcell's thin nag, knocking them down. The one-eyed bowman stood behind Burcell's horse. Redcrosse was on him before he could draw an arrow from his quiver. One-eye raised his bow to ward off the blow, but Redcrosse's sword cut through bow, his arm, and into his chest. The one-eyed archer fell dead. Redcrosse wheeled Telum around to face the rest of the band.

One rider on a scrawny nag ran into another in the indecision to run or fight. Dirty-Face attacked, thrusting a boar spear. Redcrosse dodged and cut Dirty-Face down with one blow. Rat-Face, in the greasy leather hat, swung an axe at Redcrosse's head. Redcrosse blocked it and cut Rat-Face from his chest to his arm. The man with the beard tied under his chin lashed out with a length of chain. Redcrosse leaned forward into the attack. The chain thumped harmless across his back. Then he struck the bearded man down with a back-handed swing of his sword. Spinning Telum around, he bolted into the man with fuzzy, blond-hair, throwing him under the warhorse's hooves.

At the start of the attack, the thin, bald man spurred blood from the side of his old nag and rode out of the village, the man with the bulbous nose in the old leather helmet close behind him. The fuzzy-haired blond and the man with the beard tied in a knot found their feet and took off after their running horses. Burcell crawled from under his fallen horse, slipped forward, and thrust at Redcrosse's back with his rusted sword. Arnax called out, "Behind you!"

Redcrosse turned his sword, thrust backward past Burcell's extended sword, and ran him through. Burcell fell from the blade with a great groan.

The farmer reappeared and wrestled down the youngest renegade before he could escape, then hauled him forward to Redcrosse, his fingers wound in his long, dirty hair. The youth cried out,

"Don't kill me, I meant no wrong!"

"Silence!" Redcrosse yelled. "Look about you! See the corpses of those you chose to run with."

With wide, panicked eyes, the boy looked around the scene, then sucked in his breath as he saw the villagers coming out and kicking the bodies of the fallen renegades.

The farmer said, "Well done, Sir Knight. They'll pluck from us no more 'cause them that ain't feeding the crows has tooken off like them same crows."

He asked Redcrosse, "What'll we do with this 'un?" He shoved the boy toward Redcrosse.

"Teach him to farm," he said. "I think he's had enough of banditry."

Una came out. Redcrosse said, "Are you well, Highness?"

"Well enough. I was in no danger."

Arnax broke in, "But those brigands might have harmed you."

"Perhaps. Perhaps not."

Una glared at Redcrosse and said, "If you're through adventuring, may we continue our journey?"

Redcrosse looked at the dying sun and said, "We'll stay here tonight. Day is at end and you can sleep on a bed."

The Widow Kearns motioned with her hands. She said, "This way, My Lady. I've a comfortable bed for you."

Una turned on her heels and went into the cottage.

The farmer said, "Ah, Sire, men can but wonder at the ways of women."

"Do you think those bandits will return?" Arnax asked.

"They'll not be back here," Redcrosse replied. "But I feel our paths will cross again."

# 6.

# THE HERMITAGE

## Beyond the Village

TRAVELING PAST THE MOUNTAIN toward the kingdom of the North Country, the long day grew hot. Redcrosse noticed his traveling companions, Una and Arnax, drank deep from the water bags. Pointing to a high hill off in the distance, he said, "There is a hermitage nearby. We can pass the night there."

Just before sunset they came to the hermit's hut. A tall man with a gray-streaked beard and dark, piercing eyes stepped out and motioned for them to come forward. He moved with the vigor of a young man. After bringing them inside, he seated Una by the fire, served them food and water, and stabled their animals while they ate. After the meal, Arnax went out to sleep on the straw of the stable. Una fell asleep in a chair next to the fire. The hermit motioned Redcrosse to follow him.

They climbed the high hill overlooking the plains stretching out toward the North Country. Clouds in the night sky boiled and rolled over the grassy way. A full moon rose, giving the darkened landscape a silver cast. Pointing toward the North Country, the hermit said, "In a few days you'll be challenged and will have to summon all the courage of who you are."

"I know nothing of who I am," Redcrosse replied. "I was brought to Her Majesty's court as a small child. I don't even know my name."

"A dark Faerie took you when you were in swaddling clothes."

Redcrosse's head snapped around. The hermit went on,

"You'd be slave to that same wicked Faerie, had not Queene Gloriana intervened. She caused you to be found by a ploughman—the one who brought you to court as a babe."

"And this, how do you know?"

"That's not important. You'll soon be tested."

"I was tested a day ago and near failed miserably."

"Ah, the encounter with Archimago."

"Is there anything you know not of?"

"Learn to listen to the voice of your heart."

"What does that mean?"

"Men's hearts have been turned by greed, hate, and lust. They've lost purity of spirit."

The hermit showed Redcrosse a small stone and passed it to him.

"Crush this stone," he said.

Redcrosse squeezed and squeezed.

"I can't crush stone," he said.

The hermit took the stone, pinched it, and the dust fell from his fingers.

"You believed you can't crush stone," he said. "In truth, it was but a clot of dirt."

"It was a trick then."

"No trick. Trust your senses but learn to look with your heart as well as your eyes."

"How, Friar?"

"Other men fall and rise and then fall again."

"I am no different from other men."

"Yes. And no."

"You speak in riddles."

"It falls on you to unravel these riddles."

"I'm like one casting darts in the dark."

"Answers come with time."

"How can you learn that which you're not taught?"

"Look within yourself."

"I feel like a small boy at times."

"Truth dwells in innocence."

"What I have to do can't be done by a child."

"The child David slew the giant, Goliath."

"I heed your words, but I don't understand them."

"Then, that'll have to do for now."

"That's what Her Majesty said when she gave me my weapons."

"This dragon is from an ancient evil—wiser than you know."

"You speak of the beast as though he were a man."

"Its craft and power are beyond mere mortal limits."

"Then, how will I defeat him? I'm only one man."

"Evil fears nothing but good."

"It'll take more than being good to bring down this foe, Friar."

"You mean your skill with weapons."

"I've been trained."

With a quick movement, the hermit swept both of Redcrosse's feet from under him with the end of his staff. When Redcrosse fell, the hermit leaned over him and said, "There's little I could tell you of arms."

Without a word, Redcrosse picked himself up. The hermit asked him,

"Do you know why you wear the bloody cross upon your breast?"

"No. These arms were given to me when Her Majesty knighted me. I've worn them since."

"Do you know why Her Majesty named you The Redcrosse Knight?"

"No."

The hermit traced the design on Redcrosse's tabard with his finger.

"The bloody cross, the old symbol of the sun, signs the joining of might and right. Force spawns power, but without honor, valor, and duty— the points of righteousness—power breeds evil. The blood red that colors the cross denotes virtue. They gave you gifts—seven in all. Of all these talismans, the greatest is the one you wear over your heart."

"What do I do then?"

*"Evil fears nothing but good."*

"Go and fight the good fight. And do so with all of your heart."

# 7.

# THE CHALLENGE

## On the Plains

LEAVING THE HERMITAGE, Redcrosse glanced back at the tiny figure of the hermit on top of the high hill. The road twisted in and out of the rolling plains. Near midday, Redcrosse stopped by a grove of trees near a stream to water the horses and noticed two knights dressed in seemingly identical apparel approaching.

One man wore a gray tabard imprinted with the face of a weeping woman in dark brown. The other wore a dark brown tabard imprinted with the face of a weeping man in gray.

When the two dismounted, Una gasped. They were identical twins with dark black hair and brown eyes. They saluted Redcrosse and Una. The man with the brown tabard spoke first,

"Hail, Sir Knight. I'm Sir Sansfoy."

"I'm his brother, Sir Sansjoy," the man in the gray tabard said.

"I'm the Redcrosse Knight and this is Princess Una."

"Where are you bound?" Sansjoy asked.

"To the North Country on quest for Her Majesty," Redcrosse said.

"What is your quest?" Sansfoy asked.

"I'm to relieve the kingdom from a dragon."

Sansfoy said, "A dragon!"

"Would you join us?" Una asked.

"No, Princess," Sansjoy replied. "Other duties preclude such action."

"Too bad we can't add a pair of blades to your fight," Sansfoy said.

"We'll manage," Redcrosse said.

Noticing the shield hung on Telum's flank, Sansfoy said, "What a marvelous shield."

His brother added, "And look at that lance. The blade is as long as a dagger."

Sansfoy pointed at Redcrosse's sword, he said, "What a wonderful sword! It looks very sharp."

Sansjoy patted the big horse. "Even your mount is extraordinary. And what beautiful spurs."

"Brother, look at his helmet," Sansjoy said. "I've never seen cross straps over the crown. It must be most useful."

"You are indeed well equipped," Sansfoy said.

"Perhaps you can tell us what lies ahead," Redcrosse said.

Sansjoy answered, "The way's clear."

His brother added, "Clear indeed,"

"Will you stay for a while?" Una asked.

"Alas," Sansjoy said. "We must be going on."

"Yes," Sansfoy added. "Journey well."

The two mounted and rode away.

Una stared after them.

"Those two gave me a bad feeling," she said.

"Why?"

"They never looked you in the eye and fawned over your things."

"I found their manners wearisome, but they likely meant no harm."

"I felt they're dark knights."

"Let us be on our way, Highness."

Redcrosse mounted Telum and they departed. Una did not mention the two knights again.

That evening when the party made camp, Una and Arnax fell asleep. Redcrosse lay awake long into the night.

Coming out of the clearing the next day, Redcrosse saw the two knights positioned in the road in front of them. Both were on horseback, helmets on and shields up. Redcrosse said, "In the name of our Queene, let us pass."

Sansjoy called out, "You may not pass until you have met us in combat."

"Allow us to go by," Redcrosse said. "We're on our Queene's quest."

Sansfoy replied, "No, you will not pass until you've fought us."

"I'll meet you on a fair field and fight each of you singly," Redcrosse said.

Sansfoy called back, "Agreed."

Sansjoy reined his horse to one side.

Redcrosse reached for his helmet and shield.

"Are you mad?" Una cried out. "They're two and you're one! We must get to the North Country!"

"I've been challenged, My Lady."

"I'm not your Lady and this is foolishness. We've no time to delay for some silly games."

"This is no game."

"This is man's folly."

"If I am defeated, they can claim my armor and weapons."

Using his name for the first time, she said, "Redcrosse. You can't do this. My father's kingdom is at stake."

"And so is my honor."

"What honor is there in stupidity?"

"I have been challenged on the field of honor. I must respond."

Una spat out, "I leave you to your honor! I don't know what we will do, but I'll go on alone. God knows our kingdom can fare no worse than with someone like you."

She urged her donkey past Redcrosse and rode out to the two men in the road. She called out, "Let me pass!"

Sansjoy replied through his visor, "Pass, Highness. Our fight is with him."

"The way of men defies description!"

When Redcrosse picked up the *necator draconis,* Sansfoy called out, "No! That's unfair to use that lance."

Redcrosse dropped the lance, drew his sword, brought

Telum up, raised his sword in salute. Sansfoy faced him with his lance in its holder.

They charged at the same time. At the last moment, Redcrosse reined out, taking the attack at an angle. Sansfoy's spear broke on his shield and Redcrosse knocked him from the saddle with a sword stroke. Sansfoy fell and lay on the ground.

Redcrosse circled, turned to face Sansjoy who pulled a mace from his saddle, circled, and attacked from the side. Redcrosse pushed the mace blow aside and struck the handle in two with his sword. Sansjoy pulled his sword from the scabbard and wheeled to face Redcrosse.

Redcrosse spurred Telum into Sansjoy, swinging at his head, cutting deep into his shield. Jerking the shield free, Sansjoy tried to rip the sword from Redcrosse's hand. Redcrosse recovered his balance, but Telum stumbled and fell, throwing him to the ground.

Redcrosse rolled free and saw that Sansfoy had recovered and tripped Telum with a ball at the end of a cord. Before Redcrosse could recover, the point of Sansfoy's sword was thrust to his throat. Sansfoy called out, "Yield!"

"I will not!" Redcrosse snapped back. "You're false knights who pollute the field of honor."

"Here's talk of honor and pollution from one flat on his back," Sansjoy said.

Sansfoy yelled, "Fool! You'll feel your honor soon enough."

"Kill me dishonorably and face Heaven's judgement!" Redcrosse said.

Sansjoy dismounted and kicked Redcrosse in the side.

Holding the sword to Redcrosse's throat, Sansfoy said, "We'll worry about such judgment another time."

Grabbing his brother's hand, Sansjoy said, "If we kill him thus, it could bring bad luck. Let's leave him in the woods, tied to the trees. Let the Almighty judge the wolves or whoever else will kill him."

The two brothers seized and bound Redcrosse's hands, stripped him of his helmet, spurs and belt. They dragged him into a nearby woods where they tied his hands and feet, stretching him between two trees. Sansfoy vented his fury on Redcrosse, striking and hitting him. He panted making a gasping laugh, "Now, you look well."

"Like a plucked chicken ready for roasting," his brother said.

They mounted their horses and led Telum away packed with Redcrosse's armor and weapons. Redcrosse cried out as they rode off, "You're dark knights! I'll see you cowards again—count on it!"

Both brothers laughed and rode out of the woods.

Redcrosse tugged at the cords. The more he strained, the tighter the bonds became. He muttered, "Too strong ... need to loosen the knots ... fingers ..."

Leaning into one cord, he was just able to touch the knot with his fingertips. He strained, pulling his shoulder to the

*Redcrosse tugged at the cords. The more he strained,
the tighter the bonds became.*

point of separating. He touched the knot. He started again when he heard a low growling sound.

He looked up into a pair of tiny eyes in a scarred face. The man was over seven feet tall, dressed in ragged skins. He glared at Redcrosse.

"I hate you knights," the giant said.

# 8.

# THE GIANT

### In the Woods

"HELP ME, I'VE BEEN DECEIVED by rogues," Redcrosse said.

The huge man grabbed Redcrosse and shook him. "Shut up, dog! I hate you and your kind."

"Why punish me? I've done you no harm."

Pointing to where the brothers had left, the giant said, "You're with them. I saw you together."

"With whom?"

"Them that hurt, beat, burn. The two who look like one."

"The brothers."

"Whelps from the litter of the same bitch. Hell-hounds that laugh at your pain. But now, I've got one I'll hurt and laugh at."

"They left me here to die!"

"And die you will!"

"Don't you hear me? They cheated me, fought unfairly ..."

"Stop yelping, dog!"

"Why do you think they left me here? Why am I tied up?"

The giant stopped, stepped back, and looked over Redcrosse hanging between the two trees.

"I'm helpless," Redcrosse said. "I can do no harm."

Taking in Redcrosse's bindings, the giant muttered, "They'd bait a trap with one of their own."

"No, no! They left me."

Backhanding Redcrosse across the face, the giant said, "I'll find them."

When he disappeared into the trees, Redcrosse strained against his bonds. The cords cut into his wrists from the violent shaking. The giant returned a few moments later. Redcrosse blurted, "I told you, they're gone ..."

The giant grabbed Redcrosse, jerked him forward. "Enough! I'll break your neck."

The medallion popped out from Redcrosse's tunic.

The giant stopped. Holding the medallion in his hand, he took in the design.

"Where did you get this?" he said.

"A gift from my friend, Uther."

Hearing the name, the giant drew back. "You say 'Uther?'"

"I did."

"The Gold Dragon's Head," the huge man said. "Mark of our Lord, Protector of my family."

"Uther gave it to me."

"Did you steal this? Don't lie—I'll know if you lie."

"I don't lie. It was given by my friend, Uther."

"Tell me of Uther."

"He's my stature ... green eyes ... dark-red hair."

"Red hair?"

"Yes."

"You're not like the alikes," the giant said.

"I was ..."

The huge man broke Redcrosse's bonds like cobwebs. He caught the knight's body, threw him over his shoulder and took off with him through the darkening forest. Running through the night, the giant did not slow down.

"We go," he said. "Later, I'll hunt them."

Redcrosse held onto the big man as he ran through the falling night. The giant did not stumble, falter, or slow down. After two or three miles, he came to a hill, scrambled up the slope. And stopped in front of a brush-covered hole. He kicked the foliage aside and entered a smelly cave.

The giant eased Redcrosse onto a pile of leaves and covered him with some deer skins. He said, "Here, sleep. Later, I hunt."

Redcrosse woke the next day with a burning fever. The giant brought him some strips of dried green bark, raised his head, thrust them into his mouth, and motioned for him to chew. Redcrosse chewed the acid-sour bark, then spit out the bitter pulp. The giant handed him a leather bag filled with water.

"Drink."

Redcrosse drank, closed his eyes, and fell asleep.

Redcrosse jerked awake.

"What?"

Sitting near a fire, the giant glanced up.

"Ah!" he said. "You're awake."

Redcrosse moved slowly, deliberately, painfully. He felt weak, but the fire in both shoulders was better.

"How long did I sleep?" he said.

"All two days."

"All day?"

"Yes. I gave you soup. You just sleep."

"Where am I?"

"In the cave of Orgo."

"Orgo?"

"I'm Orgo."

"You thought I was a rogue."

"All knights I met are like them. But, the two alikes are the cruelest. They trapped me. They cut my face."

"They're dark knights with no honor."

"Soon, I'll kill them."

"We'll go together," Redcrosse said. "They cheated me."

"Where are you from?"

"From Troynouvaux."

"Is Uther there?"

"Yes, that's where I left him."

"My family serves his. His protects mine. My father told me to always love the Gold Dragon's Head."

"Do you know Uther?"

"No, only his name. The fire-hair is the mark of the family."

"Uther spoke little to me of his family."

"When you spoke of fire-hair Uther, I saw your eyes and

knew you told the truth. Only Uther would give you the Gold Dragon's Head."

"We've been friends since we were boys."

The giant handed Redcrosse a bowl of strong-smelling stew.

"How'd you meet up with the brothers?" Redcrosse asked.

"They trapped and tied me like an animal."

"Why?"

"They think some treasure is hidden in the forest. Since I live alone in the forest, they thought I knew."

"Treasure?"

"I know nothing of treasure. I live alone because people hate me."

"Why would they hate you?"

"Because I'm big. Because I'm ugly. Because I frighten people. Only the Gold Dragon's Head family treats me and my kind well. I don't want to frighten anyone. I just want to be alone in the forest."

"You've been treated badly."

"All of my family are big and live in the forest. When I grew up, I came here."

"Have you always been alone?"

"Alone is fine. I live here. No one bothered me, until they came."

"We'll find them. They won't go unpunished."

"No. I'll find them."

"You can't go alone; they're armed."

"I'm not afraid."

"Listen, my friend. I was cheated too. We'll go together."

Orgo fell silent, put his hand to his mouth.

"Tomorrow we'll go," he said.

# 9.

# EVIL PLANS

## Through the Forest

REDCROSSE TRAILED BEHIND the fast-moving Orgo searching for tracks. Spotting something on the ground, the big man said, "I know where they go."

"We've no weapons and they're fully armed," Redcrosse said.

"I need no weapons."

Further down the road Orgo showed Redcrosse a horseshoe print in the dust.

"This track is recent," he said.

Setting off at a lope, the giant ran along the trail until Redcrosse was out of breath. Orgo stopped near a large tree and looked back at Redcrosse, panting heavily.

"We rest here," he said.

"Orgo, who are these brothers?"

"Bad men. Friends of the wild-eyed, bearded one."

"Archimago?"

"I don't know his name. They do what the bearded one tells."

"Where is he?"

"I don't know where he is. But the two alikes are not far ahead."

Redcrosse followed Orgo to a fork in the trail.

"We've lost them," Redcrosse said.

Orgo strode up one fork and down the other for a short distance. Pointing to the ground, he said, "Hoofmarks!"

Coming to a wooded area along a river winding through the low, rolling hills, Orgo slowed his pace, pointed to a trail leading into the woods, and took off through the leaves and grass. Arriving at a high spot near the river, he held up his hand.

"They separate here," he said. "One went this way, the other that."

Redcrosse followed Orgo along the stream edge. The giant dropped to his knee behind a stump and peered over the embankment. From behind him, Redcrosse spotted Sansjoy's gray tabard astride Telum letting him drink on the other side of the stream. Redcrosse's helmet was lashed behind his saddle, the *necator draconis* resting in the rider's lance holder.

Giving out a great cry, Orgo sprang up from behind the stump and charged across the river. He smashed into the horse and rider, knocked them down, leapt over the horse, and grabbed for Sansjoy.

The knight rolled to one side, snatched up the *necator draconis* and thrust it into the giant's belly. Orgo grabbed the handle, ripped the lance from Sansjoy's grip, threw it over his head, and sprang at the fallen knight. Sansjoy dodged the attack, whipped out his dagger, and stabbed the big man's side. Orgo jerked the dagger from Sansjoy's hand, snapped it, tossed it, then ploughed through the water after the fleeing knight.

Reaching the bank, Sansjoy drew his sword and struck a glancing blow to Orgo's side. Orgo shook it off and renewed his attack, but Sansjoy slashed the giant across his chest.

Blood gushed down Orgo's front. He made a weak lunge, but Sansjoy pushed him aside. Orgo fell to the ground. Sansjoy stood over the prostrate giant and raised his sword over his head with both hands.

The blow never fell. Redcrosse thrust the retrieved *necator draconis* through Sansjoy's chest. The sword fell from Sanjoy's hands and he turned to his attacker, eyes wide.

"You!" Sansjoy muttered and fell dead.

Redcrosse rushed to Orgo's side. The giant murmured, "The cruel one ... dead?"

Redcrosse cradled the huge man's head. "You killed him," he said.

Orgo squeezed Redcrosse's hand, "The other ... he's worse."

The giant died in Redcrosse's arms.

An arrow whizzed past Redcrosse, striking the giant's body. Redcrosse dived, rolled to one side, and snatched up the lance. Catching a glimpse of movement, he spotted Sansfoy's brown tabard behind a bush. Another arrow flew by. Redcrosse sprinted behind a rock.

"You've murdered my brother!" Sansfoy screamed. "I'll spill your guts this day!"

Redcrosse crawled to a clump of trees, his eyes fixed on Sansfoy who was squatting and notching an arrow. Redcrosse circled through the brush and closed in on Sansfoy.

Sansfoy's attention was still fixed on the rock. Redcrosse charged across the short stretch between them. Unable to bring the bow to bear on the charging man, Sansfoy leapt behind a small oak tree. Redcrosse drove the lance into the tree. The point pierced the trunk impaling Sansfoy on the opposite side. He screamed, dropped his bow, and fell.

"Help me!" he called out.

Pulling the lance from the tree, Redcrosse kicked the bow out of reach and tore his sword, *Arety*, from Sansfoy's scabbard.

"Your fate closes today, coward!" he said.

"Don't let me die ... he wants it all ..."

"Who?"

"He wants ..." Sansfoy choked, spit blood, his eyes widening. "I'm hurt. Please, don't kill me ..."

"Who is he, Sansfoy?"

"He ..."

"What of him?"

"He'd be Emperor!"

"Of what?"

"Overall ... First, the North County ... then, Gloriana ..."

"How?"

"He'd ... he'll use the dragon ... we were surprised ... your quest ... dragon ..."

"Archimago!"

Sansfoy nodded.

"Is that why you attacked me?"

"We just wanted ... the shield ... sword ... things."

"But how will Archimago use the dragon?"

"The lamia ... She'll ..."

"Lamia? He's in league with witches?"

"Fool! He'll ..."

Sansfoy choked, gagged, and died.


Redcrosse took his weapons from the brothers' bodies.

Finding the horses, he patted his big gray. He buried Orgo near the stream at the foot of a spreading oak, said a prayer, then carved an epitaph onto the tree.

*Here, Stranger, lie the bones of*
ORGO, A Giant.
*Cruelly treated in this world.*
*He died bravely with honor.*
*Bow your head. Pray that*
*his soul may rest in peace.*


Redcrosse buried the two brothers together in an unmarked, common grave at the fork of the road.

He asked the trees, "Who is the lamia and where is Archimago?"

# 10.

# THE FENS

## On the Road

THE HUMID AIR OF THE DAY bore down on Redcrosse as he rode Telum and led the two horses. The countryside had changed from rolling hills to green-spotted marshlands and the road curved into a gully between two low hills. Beyond the road split and disappeared behind two large hills with no view of what lay ahead. Redcrosse paused, then turned left.

Rounding the edge of the hill, Redcrosse found a road leading down into a swampy fen.

The trail led straight into a wooded area blanketed with a thick mist. The smell of molding vegetation hung in the air. The dimming light of approaching dusk further limited visibility.

"Go ahead, or go back, Telum?" Redcrosse said to his horse. "It looks easiest to go through the fen."

He descended into the smelly lowland. Moss hung from the branches of twisted trees. Squat bushes and heavy undergrowth crowded between thick stands of damp-trunked trees. The steamy mist hung thick in the air. No birds or other animal sounds were audible, only the dull squish

*Rounding the edge of the hill, Redcrosse found a road leading down into a swampy fen.*

of horses' hooves on the wet ground. The dim light of the dying day darkened the descent along the tortuous path that wound deeper into the fen. Taking note of his surroundings, Redcrosse pulled up and decided to turn back.

Turning the horses around, he found he and the horses

were no longer on the original trail. They now stood on a mud-soaked path that led through thick underbrush. He could not see their tracks from the way they had come. Had he even turned around?

"Where's the trail, Telum?" he said.

The shrubbery closed in as he moved forward. He stood in the stirrups trying to get his bearings. A sudden noise in the twisted trees above startled him. He looked up. A large black vulture sat looking down at him.

"Ho, friend bird!" he called out, "It's a bit soon to feast on our bones."

Crouched motionless, the large bird watched him with unblinking eyes. Redcrosse moved farther along through the underbrush. The vulture launched itself with a heavy, lumbering motion and circled above. Through the thick foliage of the menacing trees, Redcrosse could see its shadowy figure flying and gliding directly above.

The path grew soggier and more boggish. Redcrosse dismounted and led the horses along. The ground under his feet turned into mire as he slogged along—each step a torture. Finally, a path emerged. A few yards on, it forked.

"I'm lost, Telum," he said. "We don't want to fall into a quagmire."

He cut a pole and tested the muddy ground in front of him, leading the horses and probing ahead. The horses became skittish. His hand went to his sword.

Half-hidden in the shadows of the bushes and trees, he saw a large man, his face covered with a straggly beard. His balding head was spotted with patches of sparse hair, and he wore a dirty hide around his middle and upper body. His legs and feet were bare. He reminded Redcrosse of Orgo.

The huge man rushed him with a roar, a cudgel raised over his head.

Turning aside the attack, Redcrosse slipped in the sticky, muddy soil but kept his footing. Moving through the bog, the huge man attacked again, swinging his weapon, his movement slowed by the thick mud underfoot. Pushing him aside, Redcrosse yelled, "Why do you attack me?"

The giant charged again. Redcrosse tripped him when he rushed by. The huge man fell, and Redcrosse planted his foot on the man's back, knocked the cudgel from his hand, and held the point of the sword at the nape of his neck.

"I mean you no harm!" Redcrosse said.

The big man tried to rise, but Redcrosse shoved him down with his foot and pushed the sword point closer to his neck. The giant stared up into Redcrosse's face with narrowed eyes and stopped struggling.

"Answer me!" Redcrosse said.

The man grunted.

"Do you understand me?"

A nodded reply.

"If I let you up, will you not attack me?"

A pause—followed by a slow nod.

Redcrosse stood back, placing himself between the giant and his fallen cudgel. The man came to his knees.

"You don't hurt me?" he said.

"I've no cause to hurt you. Indeed, you remind me of my friend, Orgo. Do you know him?"

"No."

"Orgo was interested in this."

Redcrosse pulled out the Gold Dragon's Head medallion. The giant's eyes opened wide.

"Do you know it?"

"Yes."

In a flash movement, the giant brushed past Redcrosse, snatched up his cudgel and disappeared into the dense undergrowth.

Redcrosse watched him go, sheathed his sword, and took Telum's bridle and the other horses' leads. Hearing a noise, he glanced up. The vulture had perched in the tree above him.

"You again," he said.

The large bird did not move.

Redcrosse found that whichever way he turned, the swamp became deeper and more impenetrable. Finding himself stuck in a mire, he let go the horses' reins and tried to free his feet from the suck of the mudhole. Then he caught his foot on a root and pitched headlong into the surrounding bushes.

His face brushed something slick, smooth, and moving. He jerked his head back as something darted past his cheek. Looking up, he saw an adder, fangs poised to strike. A whizzing blur flew past his face. An arrow impaled the adder through its mouth, pinning it to the trunk of a nearby tree.

Twisting around, Redcrosse saw a small man dressed in a light-green jerkin with a bow in his hand. He helped Redcrosse to his feet.

"Thank you," Redcrosse said. "That adder meant my death."

The man put his bow away.

"I saw how you treated the ogre," he said. "Most men would have tried to kill him."

The small man squatted at the tree where the adder was pinned, pulled out the arrow, placed it in his quiver, then taking care of the dead adder's mouth, threw it into the bushes.

"Who are you?" Redcrosse asked. "And, where am I?"

"In the fens. I am Harshall, the fen dweller."

"I've been lost for hours. Can you show me the way out?"

"Once you enter the maze of the fen, there's no escape."

"No escape!"

"None for the wicked, at least."

"The wicked?"

"Many enter the labyrinth of this fen and wander in its mire until they die."

"Why?"

"Once they come in ..."

"Is there a way out?"

"I am forbidden to show anyone the way out, but since you treated the ogre so decently, I'll give you a clue."

"A clue?"

"Listen well. I'll only say it once:

*Hand on comet,*
*eyes, four blind.*
*Leader is led,*
*the path to find."*

"Master Harshall, that makes no sense," Redcrosse said.

Redcrosse looked around. He saw only the horses and the remains of the dead serpent in the bushes. He turned, called out, "Master Harshall!"

The only sound that returned to him was that of the vulture snatching up the dead adder and flapping itself into soaring flight.

# 11.

# THE LAMIA

## In the Fen

FOR MOST OF THE NIGHT, Redcrosse pushed through dense underbrush and muddy bogs. Coming to a sandy bank in a clearing, he threw himself down on the firm, soft ground and fell into a state between sleep and awake.

He jerked awake sometime later. He looked over at his horse and asked, "What was that riddle, Telum?"

The horses did not stir from their standing sleep under the misty treetops. The moon was behind a cloud, the few stars that shone through were dim, their lights dull. Redcrosse fell into a deep sleep.

He awoke before dawn, sat up in the dim glow of the morning twilight, and looked over at the horses clipping at grass. He got up and took off their saddles and rubbed their backs with a cloth. Pulling twigs from Telum's tail, he remembered the riddle.

*Hand on comet,*
*eyes, four blind.*
*Leader is led,*
*the path to find.*

He looked over at the other two horses chomping tender shoots of grass in the predawn light.

"I wish you could tell me, Telum. I feel somehow you are key to it all."

He took some hardtack from the saddlebags, chewed it, then groomed the other two horses, saddled them, and mounted up. Finding a path on the far side of the clearing, he made quick time over the firmer ground.

Coming out of the thick underbrush into a shaded clearing, he pulled up, shocked—at the far end of the clearing he saw Una sitting alone on a rock. Redcrosse called out,

"Princess!"

She came running to him.

"Sir Knight!" she said. "Where've you been?"

"How did you get into this wretched place?"

"I was misled—I believed that man and now, I am trapped here with you."

"You came here first? I just got into this hellhole yesterday."

Bursting into tears, Una clutched onto his tabard. Shocked at her sudden emotional outburst, Redcrosse stood frozen for a moment, then took her arm and led her back to the rock. She sat down, weeping. Feeling unsure, Redcrosse stared at the weeping woman.

"Where is Arnax?" he asked.

"Dead! Slain by that evil wretch."

"Archimago?"

Una jerked up her head, eyes wide with surprise. Then,

regaining her composure, she said, "No. It was the fen keeper."

"Harshall?"

"Yes."

"Are you sure?"

"He took everything I had."

"Your donkey and other things?"

"Everything means everything, does it not?"

"I don't know what to think."

"Matters worse—we're stranded in this green hell pit forsaken by God and man."

"Harshall did give me a riddle. Perhaps it's the key to our escape."

"What riddle?"

Redcrosse recited it. Una listened to it twice.

"What does it mean?" she asked.

"The words came back to me while cleaning Telum's tail."

"Cleaning Telum's tail?"

" 'Hand on comet,' says the rime—comet; and then, 'Eyes, four blind': blind, four eyes. 'The leader led,' it goes on."

Redcrosse spun around. "I've got it!"

Una was on her feet. "What did you say?"

" 'Hands on comet.' The tail. One seizes the horse's tail. 'Eyes, four blind.' Blind. Unseeing. Both one and the horse are hoodwinked. 'Leader is led'; this must mean one lets the horse have its head; and 'the path to find,' simply alludes to the animal will lead us out of the labyrinth."

"Oh! You do have it!"

Taking out a swatch of cloth from the saddlebags, Redcrosse tore it into a strip and tied it around the eyes of one of the pack horses. Una tore another strip of cloth for a blindfold. After blindfolding the packhorse, Redcrosse turned around. Una was gone.

"Your Highness!" he called out.

"Help!"

Her voice came from the brush-covered area on the other side of the clearing. Whipping out his sword, Redcrosse ran to the thicket.

Redcrosse saw Una, holding a dagger, wrestling with Harshall.

"Help me!" she screamed.

"Release her, Harshall," Redcrosse yelled.

Giving him a quick glance, Harshall kept struggling to take the dagger from Una.

"Are you mad?" he said.

"Let her go! Now!"

"Look! What do you see?" Harshall cried out.

"You're trying to harm a woman!"

"Then you're blind," Harshall replied.

Redcrosse grabbed Harshall and stuck him with the sword's pommel. The little man fell to the ground, dazed. Redcrosse stood over him.

"Kill him!" Una screamed.

Redcrosse looked at her in surprise.

"What?" he said

"Why hesitate, fool?"

Redcrosse looked back at the stunned man on the ground. Shaking his head from pain, Harshall looked up into Redcrosse's eyes.

"Look with your heart, Knight," he said.

Glancing from the screaming woman to her reflection in the polished steel of his sword blade, Redcrosse saw a face—an ugly, wrinkled face glaring at him, eyes filled with hate and anger. Redcrosse felt a new emotion: revulsion.

The image of Una before him wavered and faded away. The hideous woman screamed again, "Kill him! Weakling! Dolt!"

Redcrosse stepped toward the woman.

"You're not Princess Una!" he said. "Who are you?"

"Duessa!"

"You're a lamia!" Redcrosse said. "You're in with Archimago!"

The crone spat at him. "I'm the one who'll destroy you!"

Moving her hand in a flash, she threw a powder in Redcrosse's face. His hands went to his face, his eyes burned. With a cry, the crone stabbed him in the chest with the dagger, then ran back toward the clearing.

Harshall called out, "Stop her!"

Redcrosse had fallen to his knees.

"I can't see," he cried out. "I'm blind."

# 12.
# DARKNESS

## In the Fen

HARSHALL RETURNED to where he had left Redcrosse. The young knight sat under a tree, rubbing his sightless eyes. The short man came over and squatted beside him.

"I couldn't catch her," he said. "She took one of the hoodwinked horses and by now is finding her way out of the fens."

"I'm responsible," Redcrosse said.

"She had you completely taken in."

"If only I'd ..."

"Enough. She's far away by now."

"Can we stop her?"

"No. I'll fetch Golio. He can staunch the bleeding in your chest."

"Mayhap, it would be better if I just died here."

"Enough self-pity! You'll live to fight another day."

"Only if my opponent is led within my reach."

Harshall dashed off into the swamp. A few minutes later, he returned with the giant. The huge man lifted the tabard and looked at the wound.

"Not bad," he said.

Placing some mold-covered moss over the bleeding wound, Golio peeked into Redcrosse's eyes, moving his hand across the field of vision. Redcrosse did not react.

The giant whispered, "Not good."

"We'll take him to the hermit," Harshall said.

The huge man lifted Redcrosse, carried him back to the clearing, and set Redcrosse on Telum's back. He handed the reins to Harshall, who mounted the other horse.

Leading Telum, with the giant following close behind, Harshall moved out into the swampy forest. Leaf-covered limbs from the low-growing, twisted trees and branches of the thick bushes parted at their coming and sprang back at their passing. They emerged from the fen and headed down the road.

"Horse!" the giant cried out.

Grazing along the side of the road, the horse raised its head, whinnied, and trotted over when the other horses neighed.

"What is it?" Redcrosse asked.

"The other horse," Harshall replied.

After looking the animal over, he said, "Duessa reckoned she would go faster on foot."

"Can we go after her?"

"She's in her element now. We'd never find her."

"How could I've been so foolish as to not know her!"

"She's deceived older and wiser men than you!"

On their way, the huge Golio trod along beside Harshall and Redcrosse.

"Why did she go into the fens?" Redcrosse asked.

"The promise of beauty and life eternal."

"What do you mean?"

"It's said there's a spring in the fens in which the Holy Grail was washed; whoever drinks and bathes in the waters of that spring will be immortal and stay forever young."

"Does it exist?"

"I've lived in the fens all my life; I've never seen it."

"Duessa believed the tale and came to find the magic spring?"

"Yes, the Spring of the Water of Life. But all she found is that once you enter the fens, you can't leave."

"Then, how did she leave?"

"She stole your key to freedom."

They rode on for the rest of the day; the giant's long strides keeping up with the gait of the horses. Redcrosse sat silent, staring ahead, unseeing. Around midday Harshall reined into a grove of trees near a stream.

"We'll refresh ourselves here for a moment, Knight. I want Golio to look at your wound."

The big man lifted Redcrosse from the saddle and carried him under the trees. The giant looked again at the chest wound and grunted his satisfaction.

"Provisions are in the bags." Redcrosse nodded in their direction. "Please use them."

Harshall took hardtack and cheese from the saddlebags and passed it around. Golio ate his share in seconds and then drank deep from the stream. Redcrosse ate only a small portion of bread and cheese.

"I've enough," he said.

"I've seen rats eat more than that," Harshall said.

"No more. Give it to the giant."

Golio wolfed the food down.

"I've failed," Redcrosse said.

"How?" Harshall asked.

"My quest cannot be done by a blind man."

"Ah, let's not bury the dog until he's dead."


They came to the hermitage after nightfall. A full moon was up, and stars filled the night sky. The hermit was waiting for them.

"Bring him here," he said.

Golio lifted Redcrosse from the horse and stood him in front of the hermit. Looking into Redcrosse's face in the moonlight, the hermit grabbed Redcrosse by the shoulder and shoved him in the direction of the path up the hill.

"Walk," he said.

Redcrosse fumbled and felt his way along the path.

"I can't see, Friar."

"Then open your eyes."

"I can't. The lamia blinded me."

The hermit prodded Redcrosse with his walking stick.

"In truth, I can't see," Redcrosse said.

"If your eyes are dim, look with your heart."

Redcrosse groped his way along the steep path up the hill.

The few times he slipped and tumbled back, the hermit made no move to assist or guide him. On each occasion, he shoved and pushed Redcrosse with his staff.

Reaching the top of the hill, Redcrosse felt his way across the summit and came to the sheer edge of the drop-off. He stopped, reached out into space over the cliff and froze.

"You stand at the precipice of the hill," the hermit said. "One step either way and you fall hundreds of feet to the rocks below."

"Help me, Friar."

"Help yourself."

"My sight has been taken from me."

"Take it back."

"How?"

"Look. Open your eyes and look."

Redcrosse groped desperately with both hands.

"I'm afraid, Friar."

"I see that. Now, look your fear in the face."

Redcrosse stared blind eyes into the night. He reached out with his hands but touched nothing. He knelt, felt the ground about him determining the edge of the cliff.

"Open your eyes," the hermit said again.

"I'm blind!"

"Only if you allow it."

Raising his head, Redcrosse felt the wind in his face. He stood tall, eyes closed tight, hands doubled into fists, gritting his teeth. Taking a deep breath, he opened his eyes. He blinked. The darkness faded. He saw the twinkling points of light in the night sky. He took in the moon over the horizon. He saw the same plain that he remembered shining in the moonlight.

"I can see!" he called out.

"Of course, you can. Duessa is a liar!"

Looking around, Redcrosse realized he stood right on the edge of the cliff. Stepping back to the safety of the hilltop, he gripped the hermit's hand.

"Thank you, Friar." Redcrosse said.

"You needn't thank me. You opened your own eyes."

"Through my carelessness, Duessa escaped from the fens."

"So?"

"I've released a great evil on the people. She's likely on her way to Archimago this moment."

"Learn from it. Now, go carry out your charge."

Redcrosse met the hermit's gaze.

"I will."

"The time has come for you to know the rest," the hermit said.

"The rest of what?"

"Her Majesty chose you for this quest because yours is a great destiny. Your father was a Saxon king. Your name is George. It means 'From the Earth.' It will be known to all men in this land in the times to come. You'll be known simply as the Redcrosse Knight until you've filled that destiny."

"I understand."

"Now, Redcrosse Knight. Go fight the good fight."

# 13.

# THE APPEASEMENT

## The Border of the North Country

ARRIVING BACK IN THE NORTH COUNTRY, Una stopped at
the stone-tower guard post at the border. Arnax knocked at
the door. An old soldier opened the door.

"Names of Saints!" he called out. "It's Princess Una.
Come in, come in. Wife, attend!"

The soldier's wife made Una comfortable in a chair near
the window.

"How are things in the kingdom?" Una asked.

"Well, there's one in the capital who says he can rid us of
the great beast," the woman said.

"Who?" Una said.

The soldier interrupted, "We hear so little news out here."

The woman went on, "Rumor has it he's a magician who
can work wonders. Since he and his friends have arrived, the
great beast has not rampaged once."

"What does my father think about this?" Una said.

Una saw the old couple exchange looks.

"Oh, Highness, we've no idea." the old soldier said.

When they left the room, Una beckoned Arnax and

whispered, "Why didn't they ask anything about Troynouvaux or the champion?"

"It seems they know more than they share."

When the couple returned, Una rose to her feet.

"We'll not abuse your hospitality further," she said. "We must continue on our way."

The old soldier protested.

"Stay, Highness," he said. "You've had a long journey and should rest."

Una motioned to Arnax to take her things out.

"I'm anxious to be home," she said.

The old soldier and his wife stood in the doorway of the tower watching Una leave with the dwarf.

"She goes," the old soldier said.

"Yes," the woman replied. "And, to what terrible fate?"

Una and Arnax spent most of the day on the road to the city. Along the way, the villagers came out, greeted them, and then retreated into their homes.

"The border guard's wife was right," Una said. "The beast has not rampaged since we left. Many have rebuilt their houses. Look. Some are even planting."

"Do you think there's any truth to what the old guardsman said about the magician, Highness?"

"Not a word. It's a riddle we'll unravel at home."

The North Country's capital lay in a valley along a river between two mountain ranges to the north and south. The outlying farmlands stretched out east and west in rolling hills, linked to the city by a web of roads and villages. The castle, with its huge, brass tower built into a hill jutting out into the river, dominated the skyline of the small city.

The setting sun reflected the dying sunlight on the castle's brass tower, casting a golden glow over the city. Una paused for a moment, taking in the scene.

"Something is different, Arnax," she said.

"What, Highness? Our city looks the same to me."

Una reflected a moment.

"No ... It's only a feeling," she said.

Coming into the city, Una noticed the townsfolk doing the same as those in the country. After greeting her, they retreated into their homes and shops, closing, and barring the doors.

Arriving at the castle, Una recognized none of the guards. Crossing into the castle and into the courtyard, she dismounted her donkey. A groom rushed out from the stables to attend her. Walking into the castle, her old lady-in-waiting came out. There were tears in her eyes.

"Oh, Mistress!" she said. "We'd hoped you'd not return."

"What do you mean, Mariah?"

The woman only put her hand to her mouth. Una heard a strange voice, "Princess Una?"

Una saw a tall knight with dark brown hair and large dark eyes approach and address her. His face bore a strange smile. He wore the red and blue tabard of her father's royal guard.

"I am," Una said.

The soldier bowed and pointed to the door with a sweeping gesture.

"I am Falanxus, the new Captain of Guards," he said. "Welcome home."

"Where is Arglwydd Larn?"

"He has retired for the evening."

"Then, where is His Majesty, my father?"

"He's inside. Please follow me."

Falanxus led Una into the castle with Mariah behind her. Una saw more strange faces among the guards. None were countrymen from the kingdom.

"Mercenaries!" she whispered.

Coming into the audience chamber, Una saw a dark-haired, bearded man in a long black robe standing with his back to her, looking out the window. A large monk, his face hidden in his hood, stood nearby. When the man turned to face her, Una gasped.

"Archimago!" she cried out.

"Ah, my dear," Archimago said. "So good to see you again."

"Where's my father?"

"He's at leisure. It seems we have a bit of unfinished business."

Una's voice rose to a shout, "Last time your monk seized me and carried me off to a cave!"

"True," Archimago said. "But, as I didn't get the chance to tell you then, it was in the best interests of your kingdom."

"What are you saying?"

"This, Princess. You're the key to saving your kingdom from the great dragon."

"I went to Troynouvaux and saw Queene Gloriana—but she sent a boy with me. I failed. How's that key to anything."

"How wise to see the Faerie Queene's folly. No. You, and you alone, will be the salvation of your kingdom."

"And they will remember you forever," Falanxus said.

Her rage building to the bursting point, "You're in my father's house," Una shouted. "Be careful how you speak."

Archimago looked at Falanxus and smirked.

"She does have a temper," he said.

"Where's my father? Tell me or I'll claw your eyes out."

"Your father's indisposed. But since you'll claw my eyes out, you'd best see him soon."

Archimago motioned to Falanxus who took Una by the arm. Una tried to tear from his grasp, but he held her with an iron grip, pushed her into the hallway.

"This way, Highness," he said.

Una struggled while Falanxus pulled her into the cellar and down the long narrow steps to the lower chamber, which was divided into six storage rooms enclosed by heavy wooden bars. Una saw her father standing behind the bars of one of the enclosures. A pair of guards sitting nearby stood when Falanxus came in. Una recognized the thin bald man and the one with the bulbous nose from the village. She called out and ran to the bars of the enclosure and cried, "Father!"

Brenin Wylle held her hands through the bars.

"I prayed you'd not return," he said.

"What has happened?"

"The deceiver came. He promised relief through spells and magic. The people brought him to me and the next thing, he and his band of rogues had taken over the castle."

"Where is Arglwydd Larn?"

"Larn and my few remaining guards are locked up down here."

Falanxus stepped forward, seized her arm.

"We must go, Highness," he said.

Brenin Wylle grabbed at him through the bars, yelling, "Take your hands from her, cur!"

Never breaking his tight-lipped smile, Falanxus said, "Don't upset yourself, Majesty."

He pulled Una away despite the loud protests of her father and the men in the enclosures. He then shoved her back up the stairs and pushed her into the audience room.

Archimago greeted Una with a display of false courtesy.

"I give you a choice," he said.

"What?"

"You will present yourself tomorrow to be a willing sacrifice for the great dragon."

"Are you mad?"

"Or your father will go in your place and I will behead you and your friend, Arglwydd Larn."

"Our people will never let you carry out these deeds!"

Archimago walked over, stared out the window.

"They'll do anything to stop the dragon," he said. "We've

convinced them the sacrifice of the King's only child is the only thing that will appease the great beast."

"But it won't!"

"It will for a time. By then, we'll maneuver the dragon into Gloriana's domain where we're rid of it forever."

"This is madness, Wizard!"

Archimago turned to face her.

"Choose, Princess. The axe man or the dragon."

Una wept. "Promise me, you'll not harm my father!" she said.

"You have my word," Archimago said. "He'll not be harmed."

"Promise on your soul!" Una screamed.

"On my soul. They'll be taken to the border and exiled into the next kingdom."

Una lowered her head. "Then, I'll go willingly," she said.

*****

Shortly before dawn two days later, a long column of farm folk, townspeople, and villagers followed the cart carrying Una to the Cave of Winds. The crowd watched Una being led to the mouth of the cave. Dressed in bishop's robes, Archimago stepped forward and spoke in a great voice,

"Princess Una, Daughter of Brenin Wylle. Do you of your own free will consent to be given up that your subjects may be free from the dragon of the North Country?"

"I consent."

Falanxus led her near the cave where a heavy chain had

been mounted in a great rock and locked the chain around her middle. Archimago intoned a prayer and the procession departed.

Una was left chained to the rock.

# 14.

# THE DRAGON

## The North Country

ASTRIDE TELUM, REDCROSSE LED the two horses across the frontier into the North Country. He stopped at the border outpost and called at the door. No one answered and he continued on. Calling at each village he passed through, no one responded.

"Seems we're alone in this kingdom, Telum," he said.

Coming to a rise in the road leading into the capital, he encountered a group of farm folk walking down the road. When they saw Redcrosse, they huddled into a small group. Redcrosse called out, "Good day, friends. Is this the way to the capital?"

The farmers clung to each other, whispering among themselves. One of the men stepped forward.

"Where do you go, Sir Knight?" he said

"To the capital to see Princess Una."

The mention of Una's name caused a buzzing among the farmers.

"Princess Una's not in the capital," the man said.

"Where is she?"

Another man said, "Truth is, Sire. She's at the dragon's lair."

A familiar voice rang out, "Sir Redcrosse!"

Arnax came running down the road. Upon reaching Redcrosse's stirrup, Arnax looked up into his face and cried out, "Princess Una is in grave danger."

"What danger?"

"That same monk who captured her in the woods has taken her to the dragon's cave."

"What!"

"The monk's now the bishop," Arnax said. "While we were gone, he came here with men-at-arms and took Brenin Wylle prisoner. He convinced the people to sacrifice Princess Una to the dragon, saying that would make the beast go away. Now he and his companions have condemned Princess to her death."

Drawing his sword, Redcrosse pressed the sharp blade to the neck of the nearest farmer.

"Where is Una now?" he demanded. "Speak, fellow!"

"She's chained at the lair of the beast!"

Arnax broke in. "He knows nothing. I'll take you to her."

Redcrosse grabbed Arnax by his collar and hoisted him to the back of his saddle.

Pointing his sword at the farmer he said, "You! Watch these packhorses. I'll deal with Archimago later!"

Redcrosse sheathed the sword and spurred Telum. The big gray's hooves pounded the turf down the road. The dwarf pointed the way up the mountain pass.

"I know a shorter way. Turn here."

Redcrosse spurred the horse up the mountain. The big gray ran with great effort until they came in sight of the pass. Seeing Una chained to the rock, Redcrosse spurred Telum up next to her, drew his sword, and split the chain from the stone.

"Redcrosse! You came!" Una cried out.

"You and Arnax seek shelter. Now!"

"But, my father ..." Una began.

Looking around, Redcrosse said,

"No time now. Feel the earth tremble? The monster comes!"

Redcrosse lifted Una to the horse's back, handed Arnax the reins, clapped Telum on the rump, and sent them down the road. He slipped the helmet over his head, took up the *necator draconis* in his hand and raised the ancient shield.

The mouth of the cave turned from black to yellow in a fiery light. Sulfur bit Redcrosse's nostrils. The heat of the blast from the cave warmed his skin.

A burst of flame flared out from the mouth of the cave, and a great rumbling noise followed along with more ground shaking. The snake-shaped head at the end of the dragon's long neck emerged from the cave.

It looked around, serpentine eyes unblinking in a head filled with rows of long teeth, sharp as daggers. Gray skin with a greenish, iridescent cast lay arranged in rows of hundreds of scales, each a shining plate marking its body. The beast pushed through the opening, moving out toward Redcrosse in a swaying motion. Flapping leathery, bat-shaped wings, it weaved like a wolf.

Redcrosse saw it was as tall as a castle's archway, its neck as long as a drawbridge chain. It arched its back and flicked its pointed tail in Redcrosse's direction. The two rows of knotty scales running down its back bristled as the beast slunk over the ground.

The dragon moved on two legs, a huge, graceful bird. Its upper limbs formed into leathered wings like an ancient, great bird of prey. As it came near, Redcrosse saw long, thin fingers forming hooked talons at the ends of the wing's crests. When it raised its body, he saw its belly made up of a mass of yellowish-plated scales.

Redcrosse kept the shield up in front of his face. The claws on the dragon's feet were as thick as his arms but his greatest concern was the fiery blast from the beast's mouth. Standing his ground, Sir Allyne's words from over the years rang in his ears, "Let your opponent commit himself first."

It did. With a burst of speed, the dragon leapt forward with a loud hiss, slashing with its claws and teeth. The dragon's attack rattled against the shield. Thrown back against the rock by the force of the charge, Redcrosse bounced off the flat surface of the rock, recovered, dashed forward, and thrust the lance into the dragon's side.

The lance's sharp blade skidded along the plates of the tough scales without penetrating, but dug a furrow in the soft, leathery lining between the scales. The dragon hissed in pain and rage.

It spun around, opened its dark mouth, and spewed out a flaming blast at its tormentor. Redcrosse dropped behind the shield. The heat of the blast burnt the ground around him. The shield deflected the flames but heated near red hot, burning his hands, his arms, and his armor of mail. He cringed from the pain.

The dragon turned to lick the gash in its side with its forked tongue. Redcrosse attacked again. The lance opened another long cut between the scales on the other side. The dragon hissed again, slashed with its long teeth. Redcrosse thrust the lance into its mouth and drew blood. The dragon shook its head, gave a short blast of fiery breath at the knight, then scurried back into the cave like a gigantic vulture.

Trying to throw the searing shield away from him, Redcrosse fell back against the flat stone surface of the mountain. He tumbled over the edge, slid down the side, and rolled into a pool of water. A loud hiss erupted from the heat of the shield and armor. Redcrosse could not touch any part of his body as he lay in the water.

Una and Arnax rode up on Telum, dismounted, and ran over to Redcrosse. He called out, "Don't touch me! I'm burnt by my shield and armor."

"Quickly," Una cried. "Take it off him."

The shield had stopped sizzling and sputtering but was still hot when they pulled him out of the water and helped him to his feet.

"There's a shelter near here," Arnax said. "We can take him there."

Helping Redcrosse onto Telum's back, they led him to a hut on the other side of the mountain.

Una and Arnax lay Redcrosse down on the floor and removed his helmet. His face was blistered from the heat. He seized the dwarf's hand.

"Arnax," he said. "Take Telum and get the other two horses. There's smith's balm in their saddlebags."

Arnax left. Una wet a cloth from the water bag and sponged his face. Her voice was gruff, "Lie still."

When she told him of her encounter with Archimago, Redcrosse fell into deep thought.

"Archimago plots to usurp power not only from your father," he said. "But from Queene Gloriana as well."

"How? Queene Gloriana's the most powerful queen in Britain. She has power and an army of brave knights."

"I don't know how. I've learned they can influence the dragon."

Una was on the verge of tears.

"What can we do?" she said. "If we run, they'll murder my father and loot the kingdom. They've deceived the people and even I played into their hands by consenting to be sacrifice to the dragon."

"You were forced by the cruelest means to consent."

A long pause. Redcrosse said, "But now the game changes."

"What do you mean?"

"Archimago's overextended his hand. The people now know I am here. They'll know too that you've not been killed. That knowledge will cast doubts on his powers. If he harms your father now, the people could revolt and ruin all his plans."

"But he has men-at-arms."

"How many mercenaries did you see at your father's court?"

"At least a dozen or so."

"That is hardly enough to put down a revolt—even if his men are well-armed. Are there any horsed knights?"

Una thought for a moment.

"Well, one," she said. "His Captain of Guards, Falanxus alone, wore spurs."

Heaving to his feet, Redcrosse walked around the little cottage.

"I've part of a solution," he said.

"What?"

"In any case. I've got to slay the dragon."

# 15.

# THE DRAGON'S WRATH

## In a Hut near the Cave of Winds

ARNAX RETURNED AFTER SUNSET with the saddlebags. Redcrosse took out the jar of balm and strips of the bark Golio had given him. Una rubbed the mixture over his burns while Redcrosse chewed on the bark. After a short rest, he said, "I'll fight tomorrow."

"Those ploughmen we met have carried the tale of your fight to their village and now they know of it in the city," Arnax said.

"How did they know?" Redcrosse asked.

"Because I told them the dragon is sorely wounded and Princess Una is alive."

"You told them the dragon was wounded?" Una said.

"Well, yes, Mistress ... sort of wounded," Arnax replied,

"He's little more than scratched," Redcrosse said. "I've likely made him madder than hurt."

"Don't tell any more untruths!" Una snapped.

"No," Redcrosse said. "But you can tell all that their Brenin is a prisoner of this Wizard pretender, Archimago."

"Easily done. I know just the right gossips to feed this knowledge to."

*****

The sun arose to a gray, windy day. Clouds rolled and turned over the mountains and plains. In the city and villages, townspeople and farm folk looked out their windows at the sky and mountains, then hurried back inside.

*****

Approaching the Cave of Winds, Redcrosse raised his lance and shield. He had wrapped Telum's head and front with thick cowhide, leaving the horse's legs and hooves unprotected to allow greater movement. Hearing movement at the cave, he pulled down his helmet and moved near the mouth of the cave.

The dragon stepped out and peered around the cave. Fixing his aim at a point between the scaly plates, Redcrosse spurred Telum. The big gray charged.

Redcrosse struck the dragon where the hard back scales joined the softer ones of its belly. The *necator draconis* pierced its side and blood spurted forth. The dragon hissed, swung its head, and raked its teeth at the horse and rider. Jerking the lance free, Redcrosse thrust again, leaving another deep gash between the scales along the dragon's back.

The dragon whipped its tail. Redcrosse reined Telum in close. The lashing tail struck the side of the mountain, throwing up a blast of dust and rocks. Redcrosse thrust the lance near the dragon's hip, piercing the flesh between the plates.

The dragon leapt away. Redcrosse bolted Telum into a crevice between the mountains. The dragon sprang and clawed at the rocks of the opening. Deep in the recess beyond the slash of the huge talons, Redcrosse backed up Telum. The dragon let go a burst of fire into the crevice. Bright red flames engulfed the passage as the horse and rider retreated out the other side. Hopping like a huge bird, the dragon jumped, soared, and lit on top of a large rock over the passageway.

Redcrosse rode around the side of the mountain staying under an outcropping shelf. Coming to the other side, he slowed Telum and looked up at the dragon above him.

The dragon's unblinking eyes glowed as they scanned for the horse and rider. Blood leaked from the wounds in its side, but it showed no sign of weakness. Then Redcrosse noticed the dragon's gaze had fixed on him and his horse. The dragon leapt into a soaring dive straight at them.

Redcrosse spurred Telum away from the dragon's attack, reined hard, and turned the big gray in a sharp turn. The dragon, slashing with its mouth, just missed the wheeling horse. Redcrosse jammed the lance into the dragon's soft underbelly.

The lance struck and stuck in its belly. The dragon arched its wings and raked its claws at the source of pain. The force of this movement tore the lance from Redcrosse's hand and pulled him from the saddle. The dragon soared to another outcropping, the lance still stuck in its belly, and snapped at the wound with its teeth.

Remounting Telum, Redcrosse saw this movement had caught the dragon's eye. It stopped clawing and dove once more at the horse and rider.

Drawing his sword and raising his shield, Redcrosse charged the dragon. At the last moment, he swerved and struck at the sweeping talons as the dragon swooped by, grasping with its claws. The sword cut through the dragon's toe and severed a talon. The dragon lit on a ledge, turned, and let fly another burst of flame at the horse and rider.

Redcrosse moved Telum to safety. The dragon shook its injured foot, leapt from the ledge and dived again at its adversary, its mouth open, teeth thrust forward.

Turning the horse into the dragon's flight, Redcrosse warded off the biting attack with the shield and sliced a long gash along the dragon's nose. The dragon spun about like a hawk in flight and seized Redcrosse with its feet.

The dragon tore Redcrosse from the saddle and soared aloft with him. Redcrosse dropped the shield and grabbed onto the dragon's foot. Held fast by the talons, he hacked at the steel-hard claws with the sword. The blade chipped pieces from the claws. A raking motion from the other claw stripped the sword from Redcrosse's hand.

Spotting the lance still stuck in the dragon's belly, Redcrosse stretched out, grabbed the handle, and thrust it again and again into the dragon's belly. The dragon shuddered, hissed, and dropped him. Clutching the handle of the lance, Redcrosse kicked and fell against the side of the mountain. Jamming the butt of the lance in the mountainside to slow his descent, he slid down the side of the slope, striking rocks and ledges, tumbled over a ledge, and came to rest at the foot of the mountain.

Later in the afternoon, Arnax and Una recovered Redcrosse's sword, shield, and Telum. They found Redcrosse still clutching the lance. Arnax called out, "Sir Redcrosse! Can you hear me?"

Redcrosse groaned and tried to sit up.

Una said, "Bring the horse up!"

Leading up the big gray, Arnax and Una pushed and heaved Redcrosse across the saddle.

"The dragon?" he said.

"Still alive," Arnax replied, "It's gravely wounded. It flew into the cave after loosening you."

Redcrosse passed out. Una cried out, "Go find the old shepherd. He'll know what to do."

Redcrosse lay on a bed of sheepskins drinking broth. The old shepherd rubbed his back and legs with oil.

"This'll put you right, Sir Knight," the old man said. "Wool oil and leaves from the tree of life."

Una gave him some leaves and herbs.

"Chew on these," she said.

"These taste like those Orgo gave me," Redcrosse said.

"It's bark from the willow tree," Una replied. "Our local people call it the Tree of Life because they believe it can revitalize the wounded."

Redcrosse drank from the offered water bag and fell asleep.

"I thought he was dead when he fell," Arnax said. "He must have been caught by an angel."

"He's all cuts and bruises," the old shepherd said. "Rest will do him well."

After the shepherd left to go back to his flock, Una sat looking at the sleeping knight. Arnax touched her arm.

"Take heart, Highness," he said. "All will be well soon."

"We still have the dragon," Una said. "We still have the usurper in my father's castle."

Arnax placed her cloak around her shoulders and said, "Rest, Mistress. I'll watch him tonight."

# 16.

# THE DRAGON'S LAIR

## At the Cave of Winds

THE STILL AIR BORE THE SCENT of burnt sulfur. Redcrosse gripped his spear handle. It was made of tightly twisted root fibers smoothed into a steel-hard smoothness by file and fire. It felt good in his hand. Anticipating action, the big gray warhorse bobbed his head, switched his tail and stamped his hoofs.

"Today is the day of accounting, Telum," Redcrosse said.

The dragon poked its head out of the cave, looked both ways, and crept out. The marks of the previous day's battle showed in dark purple patches on its gray-green skin, but he had no loss of agility.

Keeping in the dark shadow of the mountain, Redcrosse held the great warhorse back. The dragon darted forward looking to the left and right. When it turned its head, Redcrosse spurred Telum and charged.

The dragon swung its long neck around to meet the attack. Redcrosse stuck the dragon where the wing joined its shoulder. The sharp spear blade slit the flesh at the joint, leaving the wing dangling in a stream of blood. The dragon slashed at its antagonist with its open mouth, striking only open air.

Redcrosse rammed the lance in the side, between the dragon's scales. Blood spurted from the wound. The dragon wheeled, lashed with its tail. Redcrosse reined in next to the dragon's body, away from the whip of the tail, and drove his spear into the dragon's leg.

Tail lashing, teeth slashing, feet mashing in fury, the dragon let go a burst of fiery breath at its attacker. Staying close to its side, Redcrosse thrust the spear, cutting a long, deep gash between the scales along its flank. The dragon slung its body trying to pin horse and rider against the side of mountain. Redcrosse spurred Telum under the dragon's neck and bolted for the narrow crevice near the mouth of the cave.

Glancing back, Redcrosse saw the dragon retreating into the cave. It hobbled now. Blood dripped from several wounds. The wounded wing drooped at its side.

Redcrosse dismounted, took lance and shield, and ran to the cave. Inside he found a passageway that opened into a large grotto. He stopped, letting his vision accustom to the dark. In the dim light, he saw bones and debris strewn over the grotto floor. Searching around for a sign of the dragon, he caught sight of a dark hole at one end leading into the cave's interior.

Going up to the mouth of the hole, he peered in. There was no light. He could see nothing. Prodding in front of him with the end of the lance, he made his way in.

A noise!

Dropping to his knee, he threw his shield up and flattened himself against the cave's wall.

Closing his eyes and straining his ears, he heard the sound again. Estimating its origin as coming from his left, he set the lance and shield on the ground, groped around, found a jagged stone the size of an orange, leaned back, and threw it in the direction of the noise, then snatched up lance and shield, rolled to his right, and fell behind it.

A burst of flame lit up the cave. He had hit the dragon with the stone. The fiery blast scorched the cave wall next to him. Now he saw the dragon was only a few feet away.

Redcrosse jumped up and thrust the lance at the dragon. The blade skidded off its tough scales. He thrust again, again, and again. He felt the blade pierce something soft. The dragon gave out a hissing shriek and burst forth, knocking Redcrosse down and rushing back into the dimly lit grotto.

Recovering his lance and shield, Redcrosse dashed into the grotto where he saw the dragon clawing and lashing at shadows. Redcrosse had pierced one of its yellow, serpentine eyes. He attacked from the dragon's blind side and jabbed the lance into the soft underbelly.

Lashing out with its tail, the dragon knocked Redcrosse across the grotto. He fell against the rock wall but managed to scramble behind a rock outcropping when the dragon shot another fiery blast. Redcrosse crawled from behind the rocks to a spot near the mouth of the dark passageway. The dragon jerked its head, sending blasts of flame in all directions.

Snatching up another stone, Redcrosse hurled it. The stone clattered past the dragon and it sent a burst of fire in that direction.

Redcrosse scrambled forward and scooped up the lance and shield. The dragon whipped its neck around and slashed with its open mouth. Fending off the attack with his shield, Redcrosse thrust up with the lance catching the dragon in its throat.

Smelly, oily matter spurted from the throat wound. Coughing, gagging, the dragon hacked out another burst of flame—tiny, with little effect. Redcrosse jabbed the spear at the dragon's mouth but the beast knocked him down with its lashing tail.

The dragon backed away, focused on Redcrosse, and spat out a fire-burst with flames no bigger than a campfire. Redcrosse warded off the weak burst with his shield. The dragon wheeled and scrambled out of the cave.

Redcrosse chased the dragon out into the sunlight, stopping for a moment and shielding his eyes from the strong light. The dragon spun around and raked him with its mouth, knocking him to his knees, then tried to trample him.

He rolled aside, sprang up, raised his shield, held his lance in position, and circled the dragon. The great beast turned and tried to blast him, but generated only small, weak flames. It clawed at Redcrosse, but its attack bounced off his shield.

The dragon exposed its belly. Redcrosse charged, stabbing the lance into the beast's chest. Redcrosse thrust again and again. The dragon gasped a choked hiss. It fell.

*Redcrosse thrust up with the lance catching the dragon
in its throat.*

Drawing out the lance, ready to thrust again, Redcrosse held up.

The dragon was dead.

Covered with blood, the lance in his hand, he let the shield slip from his arm and dropped the *necator draconis*.

He heard Una's voice,

"It's dead!"

Redcrosse turned to see Una, Arnax, and the shepherd coming behind him.

"You've killed it!" Una called out.

She stopped, looked at his bloody figure.

"You're hurt!" she cried out.

In a flat, empty voice, he said, "No. It's dragon's blood."

"You saved us!" Arnax cried. "The terrible beast is dead."

"Now we can live in peace," the shepherd said.

Redcrosse looked over at them, then gazed at the dead dragon.

"It was a noble beast," he said. "I think the only evil it committed was that which men forced it to do. It fought bravely and died terribly."

"It ravaged and killed!" Una cried out. "Don't mourn it to me!"

"I don't."

Redcrosse sat down, removed his helmet, and continued to stare at the dead dragon.

"So, help me, part of me laments that I had to kill it. We don't know where it came from or why it came here."

"What do we do now?" Arnax asked.

Still looking at the fallen reptile, Redcrosse said, "We have to rescue the Brenin."

"How?" Arnax asked.

Redcrosse walked apart from them. He looked up at the mountaintops and caught sight of a soaring hawk. Coming back next to the fallen dragon, he said, "We must think like Archimago."

# 17.

# THE OTHER DRAGON

## The Cave of Winds

THE NEXT MORNING, REDCROSSE led Una, Arnax, and the old shepherd to the Cave of Winds. The remains of the slain dragon were gone. Only a large blotch of burnt, ash-covered earth remained.

"It's gone!" Arnax said.

"Has it risen from the dead?" the old shepherd asked.

Redcrosse looked over the patch of ground covered in ashes.

"Are you sure it was dead?" Una said.

"The beast was dead," Redcrosse said. "It has not risen from the dead. I see the hand of Archimago in this."

*****

In the capital, the guardsmen of Archimago, now Bishop Regent, called the citizens of the North Country to a public hearing. The people gathered in the great square in front of the castle with the brass tower. They whispered among themselves in frightened voices, spreading rumors about the dragon and Princess Una that changed with each telling.

Wrinkling his face and scowling at those around him, an old peasant stepped apart from the crowd, "I don't like this talk," he said in a loud voice. "Me and m'father before me served the family of good Brenin Wylle. He never asked this hellish monster to come here and I'll not hear ill of 'im today."

Several people stopped their muttering, turned, and stared at the old peasant. His daughter whispered, "Hush, old father, there are ears and tongue-wags about."

"I don't care either!" the old man snapped back. "I don't believe none of it anyway."

Several people standing near the old man turned their backs to him and resumed whispering in low, buzzing voices. The bishop's men-at-arms walked up. The whispering stopped. The old man's family moved him away from the glares of the armed men.

The thump of a large drum sounded. Dressed in his bishop's robes, a miter on his head, a bishop's crook in his hand, Archimago strode out of the tower door followed by Brother Typhon, his face hidden in the cowl of his cassock. When Falanxus led Brenin Wylle, under guard, to the center of the landing, a great gasp let out from the crowd. Brenin Wylle's hands were bound behind his back, but he held his head high, eyes defiant.

Archimago called out, "Citizens of the North Country! I stand here on a sad occasion."

He walked to the front of the group and pointed at Brenin Wylle.

"This man who pretends to be your sovereign has deceived you greatly," he said. "For his own greed and avarice, he caused this terrible beast to come and destroy your homes, your crops, and your peace. His nefarious purposes remain known but to him and the evil one."

Archimago swaggered across the square, swinging his hands in sweeping gestures.

"Alas, in the attempt to attain their wicked ends, he caused the death of his only daughter. However, her sacrifice may have undone the evil wrought by their conspiracy. In our ecclesiastical court, we've heard great evidence against them. It is our judgment that he be brought here before you for punishment. He will be beheaded for his terrible crimes against you."

Angry murmurs arose from within the crowd. The people pressed forward, raising their hands in protest. The men-at-arms moved in closer to Archimago. He held up his hands for quiet.

"I understand your concerns and loyalty," he said. "But you've been victimized and suffered much. Now the time comes for justice."

A voice rang out from the back of the crowd, "Liar!"

Princess Una pushed her way to the front of the crowd, followed by Arnax and the shepherd.

"Fiend!" she screamed. "Your words are as false as the bishop's miter on your head."

Archimago raised his face and bishop's crook to the sky.

He cried out, "Be praised, ye heavens above. The Princess Una lives!"

Una's anger was at the point of rage. She said through clenched teeth, "You perjure yourself, Sorcerer. You left me chained at the Cave of Winds to die."

"Only because you went there of your own free will. These good people heard you consent."

Una's eyes burned above the veil.

"Those words were forced from me," she said. "You swore upon your soul that my father would not be harmed if I went to the rock."

"But the dragon has gone, Dear Lady. Your humble sacrifice, however wrought, made the monster go away."

"You lie, Wizard."

A tall man in a cloak stepped out of the crowd. Throwing off his cloak, the blood-red cross stood out on his white tabard in the morning light. Stepping up to Archimago, he thrust his finger in the false bishop's face.

"The dragon's gone because I killed it," he said,

Archimago and the men-at-arms burst into laughter.

"It's true!" Una cried out. "I saw it with my own eyes. So did Arnax and the shepherd."

Voices among the crowd grew louder. Cries of disbelief and the noise of confusion rose throughout the gathering. Archimago laughed, shook his head, and opened his arms wide.

"Child, we all know you'd say or do anything to save your

father. But lying ill becomes you. And, as to the quality of your witnesses ... well, your servant and this fellow?"

"We were there, Wizard!" Arnax called out. The shepherd nodded and looked around.

"Truly, friends," he said. "You know I never lie. We saw the Redcrosse Knight slay the beast."

"Come now, Princess," Archimago said. "You'd have us believe this deluded young man alone killed the great dragon?"

"He indeed killed the dragon!"

Archimago stiffened. His manner changed. Pointing his finger at them, he thundered, "Tell us, and you too, Sir Knight, where are the dragon's bones?"

Archimago turned to face the crowd.

"Whom will you believe?" he said. "This girl who'd risk the fires of hell to save her wicked father. These servants of hers? Or perhaps, you'd believe this stranger—this foreigner who appears out of nowhere and declares 'I killed the dragon.'

"Where were they when your crops were burning? Where did they hide when your livestock and even your children were given up to the insatiable appetite of this ungodly monster?"

Archimago strode across the front of the square, waving his bishop's crook. He spun around and pointed at the crowd.

"Nay! The monster's wrath was stayed by our holy intervention. Now they come here to lead you astray when it is safe, and the voice of justice is about to be heard."

Archimago paced in front of the crowd. "Return Brenin Wylle to the throne, say you? So, he can bring more dragons? Remember, Brenin Wylle allowed this behemoth to wreak destruction on you. He can just as easily bring another!"

"No, no!" a voice from the crowd cried out. "No more dragons." The crowd picked up the cry and chanted, "No, no, no!"

Redcrosse called out, "Citizens of the North County! I am the Redcrosse Knight, sent here with Princess Una by Her Majesty, Queene Gloriana, the Faerie Queene. I was charged to slay the dragon and I did."

"This man is not a bishop of our Holy Mother Church. He's a rogue and deceiver. Last night, the dragon's remains were burned in front of the Cave of Winds. I suspect this liar had much to do with that."

"How convenient," Archimago said. "He slays the dragon, then suddenly, mysteriously, it disappears? A great dragon! As tall as this tower! Who's the liar here?"

Pale with anger, Redcrosse shouted, "I do not lie, Wizard."

"Enough," Archimago said, "Carry out the sentence."

Brother Typhon picked up an axe, grabbed Brenin Wylle, and pushed him forward. Una screamed and ran to him but one of the armed guards grabbed her.

Redcrosse yelled, "Hold!" He threw his glove at the feet of Archimago.

The noisy crowd became still. Archimago looked at the gauntlet in front of him and then at Redcrosse.

"What's this?" he asked.

"A glove, Wizard. Pick it up."

"You can't challenge me." Archimago said. "I wear the cloth of the Church."

Redcrosse called out, "I claim the right of trial by combat for Brenin Wylle. Here in front of these people, will you deny the Brenin's right to defend himself by arms? Let God be his judge!"

Archimago's face turned crimson.

"Carry out the execution!" he snapped.

"Nay." The voice of the old peasant rang out, "It's Brenin Wylle's right. Trial by arms! Let God judge!"

The crowd took up the cry. Voices from all rang out, "Arms, arms, trial by arms. May God judge!"

The noise grew and the people moved toward the square shaking their fists and shouting. The men-at-arms glanced over at Archimago who looked around himself and once more at the glove lying in front of him. Pointing to the gauntlet, Redcrosse said, "Take up the challenge or release the King."

Falanxus strode forward, snatched up the glove, and hurled it back to Redcrosse. Once again, a hush fell over the square.

Archimago nodded to Falanxus and stepped back.

"Your challenge is accepted," Falanxus said.

Una broke free and ran to embrace her father.

Redcrosse said to Brenin Wylle, "Your Majesty. Am I an acceptable champion?"

"If I were younger," Brenin Wylle replied, "I'd teach these dogs to bark a different tune myself."

Redcrosse cut his bonds and Brenin Wylle turned to the crowd and said, "I accept this man as my champion!"

Archimago sneered and strode to the center of the square.

"Well, then," he said. "At the rising of the sun tomorrow, Brenin Wylle's champion, the Redcrosse Knight, will meet the champion of justice, Sir Sansloy."

Hearing the name, Redcrosse looked into the face of Falanxus. He whispered, "The brothers—the same dark eyes, the same dark hair ..."

Pointing her finger at Falanxus, Una cried out, "You're a dark knight!"

Falanxus replied, "Falanxus is but a nickname. I'm the youngest of a family of three great warrior knights."

He looked over at Redcrosse. The little smile became a sneer.

"Pray well tonight, vassal," he said. "Tomorrow will be your last day on earth."

# 18.

# TRIAL BY COMBAT

## The Castle of the North Country

BRENIN WYLLE SAT WITH UNA and Redcrosse after supper as a guest in the home of a loyal merchant for the night.

"Larn and my loyal guards still rot in the dungeon," he said.

"They'll be free tomorrow, Majesty," Redcrosse said.

"Aren't you worried about their champion?" Una asked.

"Until we can prove I killed the dragon, there'll be doubt in the minds of the people and fertile ground for Archimago in the future," Redcrosse said.

"What happened to the dragon's remains?" Brenin Wylle said.

"Archimago must have burned it," Redcrosse said. "He was too well prepared for us today."

"What can we do?" Una asked.

"In the fight I severed one of the dragon's talons. Arnax and the shepherd are searching for it. Finding and bringing it here will offer tangible proof."

"It's but scant proof," Brenin Wylle said.

"True. But it's all we have," Redcrosse said.

People crowded into the square in front of the tower long before dawn. Brenin Wylle and Una took seats on the side opposite the tower. Redcrosse sat on Telum in front of them, the *necator draconis* resting in his lance holder.

The drawbridge from the castle lowered, the door to the tower opened, and the mercenaries fanned out in front of the crowd. Archimago strode about in his bishop's robes blessing the crowd. Coming out last, on a dark horse followed by his seconds, Falanxus Sansloy wore a checkered tabard over his dark armor in the same brown and gray as his brothers. A face, half man and half woman, in a weeping attitude, was etched on the tabard's breast. The arms on his shield were of the same color and pattern.

Archimago walked to the center of the square, postured, and rapped his bishop's crook for attention.

"Citizens of the North Country," he said. "We're here to determine guilt or innocence of the crime of consorting with the Unholy One—in spite of a court of inquisition having already found the Brenin guilty, he'll be defended by that knight."

Archimago pointed to Redcrosse. He then motioned toward the large figure of Typhon who stood holding the axe, his face still hidden in the cowl of his cassock.

"The right and might of our Holy Office are vested in this knight, Sir Sansloy," he said. "When he wins, death by beheading of the guilty will be carried out immediately. Do you understand this, Brenin Wylle?"

Brenin Wylle stood and answered, "I do."

"Sir Knights," Archimago called out, "draw near."

The two knights came to the center of the square. The blood-red cross on Redcrosse's tabard and shield stood out in the light of the rising sun. Archimago looked at Redcrosse.

"There'll be no quarter," he said.

"Expect none," Sansloy added. "And, I'll not yield."

"So be it," Redcrosse answered. "I've seen how your kinsmen fight."

Sansloy's dark eyebrows knit into a frown. "What do you mean?"

"I engaged in combat with your twin brothers," Redcrosse replied. "Both were villains and fought foul. I killed and buried them both."

Sansloy's horse twitched and moved about from the tension of the rider. He shouted, "Liar!"

"I don't lie, Sansloy," Redcrosse said. "I tell you again. I slew both of your brothers, Sansjoy and Sansfoy."

Sansloy's face went pale. He screamed again, "Lies! All lies!"

"Sansjoy died killing my unarmed friend and Sansfoy died in my arms," Redcrosse said. "Before he died, he revealed the plans of this false man." He pointed at Archimago.

Archimago ignored the remark. Sansloy's dark eyes, blazed at Redcrosse for a moment. He became quiet, his cold smile returned. He patted the neck of his dark charger, calming him. His voice hissed like an adder's, "Hear me! One of us dies this day—I intend it be you."

He clamped down the visor on his helmet and rode to the end of the square.

Archimago leered at Redcrosse. He asked, "Do you want God's blessing?"

"Not from you, Dog of a Wizard."

"Then go with the stain of sin on your soul."

Archimago wheeled around and took a seat in front of Brother Typhon.

Una called out, "Redcrosse!"

He came to her and extended his lance. She removed her veil and tied it on the end of the *necator draconis*.

"Please, wear my colors," she said.

Redcrosse clapped on his helmet, rode to the end of the square, raised his lance, and saluted his opponent. Sansloy charged without returning the salute. Redcrosse lowered his lance and spurred the big, gray horse.

The two horsemen met headlong. Redcrosse took the point of Sansloy's lance in the center of his shield. It shattered on impact. The *necator draconis* tore through Sansloy's shield, ripping it from his grasp, cutting across his arm. The agile Sansloy kept his balance, threw away the broken spear and shield. Taking up a morning-star mace from his saddle, he swung the spiked ball at the end of the chain around his head and moved his dark horse in a circle to Redcrosse's left.

Redcrosse rode back to the end of the square and dropped the *necator draconis*. Whipping out his sword *Arety* he turned back to face Sansloy. Redcrosse blocked a swing of the mace on his shield and cut back at Sansloy's head, slicing off an ornament from the top of his helmet.

Sansloy reined away, rode to the other side of the square, and seized up another shield. Attacking, he dodged a sword cut and whipped the mace's ball over the shield. The ball struck the cross-bands on Redcrosse's helmet and bounced off. Redcrosse reined out, shook his head from the shock of the blow, and turned back to Sansloy.

The two men fought the entire morning. The sun was nearing the point of midday. Both showed the strain. Attacks were slower, more deliberate, blows less frequent, with more frequent rest breaks, and longer. Both lathered horses were breathing as hard as their riders.

Sansloy moved in, feinted a blow at Redcrosse, and swung instead at Telum's head. Redcrosse ignored the feint and struck the ball of the mace with his sword, deflecting it from the horse. He spurred Telum straight into the dark charger. The big gray hit the dark horse with his chest at the front shoulder and knocked it over backward.

Rolling free of the falling horse, Sansloy scrambled to his feet. Redcrosse reined the big gray out, dismounted, and faced Sansloy on the ground. They circled, weapons and shields raised. Sansloy swung the mace, catching Redcrosse's shield on the top edge. The shield moved out of line from the force of the blow; Sansloy wheeled the weapon and whipped the ball into Redcrosse's shoulder. The white of the tabard colored red from the impact of the spiked ball, but Redcrosse stepped into Sansloy, preventing a second swing.

Sansloy renewed the attack, striking the lower edge of the shield. In spite of his wound, Redcrosse clutched onto the ancient shield. Sansloy struck again at his opponent's head. Redcrosse stepped in, riposted, cutting across Sansloy's shield, and split it. Redcrosse pulled out the blade and cut the other side, rending the shield in two pieces. Sansloy threw the useless shield aside and attacked, swinging the mace with both hands again and again. Falling back from the onslaught, Redcrosse caught one of Sansloy's blows to his side but then shot his sword hand in a straight punch to Sansloy's face. The pommel of the sword caught Sansloy square in the faceplate and knocked his head back. Redcrosse lunged forward, drove his sword hand in a blow to Sansloy's chest, and he fell flat on his back.

Redcrosse stepped on the mace, stuck his other foot on Sansloy's chest, reached over, and loosened the chin strap. He ripped the helmet from Sansloy's head and pushed the point of his sword at Sansloy's throat.

Out of the corner of his eye, Redcrosse saw Archimago make a signal. Without hesitating, Redcrosse brought the shield up. An arrow bounced off. He cried out to the prostrate man in front of him, "Yield!"

With the sword point at his throat, the pale Sansloy did not struggle; he looked up at Redcrosse, eyes full of fear.

"I yield!" he choked out. "You've won!"

A roar of cheers blared from the crowd and surged forward.

Hesitating, Archimago's men-at-arms looked from one to the other. Redcrosse stepped back and faced Brenin Wylle and Una. He felt motion behind him and spun around. Sansloy had recovered the mace and now raised it over his head to strike.

Redcrosse stepped into Sansloy and ripped the weapon from his hand. Sansloy drew his poniard and thrust it into Redcrosse's side. Redcrosse struck him across the head with his own mace. Sansloy reeled back, fell, stared up at Redcrosse, tried to say something, and died.

"Foul," Archimago yelled, "Foul play! You slew an unarmed man after he yielded."

His men ran up and surrounded Redcrosse, weapons extended. Redcrosse saw the four renegades among them that had fled the village.

"In the name of honor, give up your weapon, Knight!" Archimago cried out.

Voices from the crowd yelled in angry protest. People surged forward onto the square. The men-at-arms looked back to Archimago standing shocked by this sudden change of events.

Redcrosse laughed. He pulled off his helmet. He stopped laughing. His eyes blazed.

"'In the name of honor!'" he said. "You take us all for fools."

His voice weaker now, Archimago screamed, "Give up your sword!"

Redcrosse looked around at the men-at-arms. "Come and take it!" he shouted. "Who'll be the first?"

The men-at-arms looked over their shoulders, first at Archimago screaming at them to attack, then at the angry crowd pressing in, shaking their fists and yelling, then back at Redcrosse, standing with Sansloy's morning-star mace in one hand and his own sword in the other.

A strong voice rang out, "Stand!"

With Una behind him, Brenin Wylle pushed his way through the crowd.

"These two went last night to find remains of the dragon," he said. "They've returned with the proof that the Redcrosse Knight has slain the great beast."

Arnax and the shepherd came forward, holding up the severed claw of the dragon. Archimago screamed, "It can't be! Duessa burnt it completely."

Several people in the crowd gasped. Cries and murmurs erupted,

"Oh no!"

"What?"

"They were right!"

Una thrust her fist in Archimago's face.

"We know now, Sorcerer," she said.

Archimago grabbed her and forced her head back with the bishop's crook staff against her throat.

"Back!" he yelled. "Back to the tower. Now!"

His men-at-arms withdrew, holding out their weapons to keep the advancing crowd at bay. The men-at-arms, backed by the big, hooded monk covered Archimago's retreat as he dragged Una across the drawbridge into the brass tower. The portcullis slammed down, the tower door clapped shut, and the drawbridge rose while angry people pelted the tower with stones.

"Can we get in there?" Redcrosse asked.

The castle stood on a hill at the edge of a river, a moat surrounding the structure and connecting back to the river, making it an island. Brenin Wylle pointed Redcrosse's attention to a rock formation jutting out from the far side of the castle.

"Under that outcropping is a way into the castle," he said. "Arnax can show you the way in."

# 19.

# THE KEEP

## Inside the Castle

UNA PUSHED AGAINST THE HANDLE of the staff in an effort to breath. She saw her father and Redcrosse at the head of the crowd before the drawbridge rose up and the portcullis slammed down. Once inside, she felt Archimago turn his head and heard his voice, "To your posts!"

Una kicked Archimago with her heel on the inside of his leg below the knee and pushed the staff from her throat. The Wizard cried out, "Foul wench! I'll teach you!"

He grabbed her chin and tried to twist her neck. Una bit his hand, sinking her teeth in as hard as she could. Archimago let out a cry of pain and released his grip. Una spun around and kneed him in the groin. When he doubled over from the pain, she sprinted off toward the stables.

Gasping for breath, holding his bleeding hand, Archimago called out, "Catch her!"

The guards stood in shock at the sudden confrontation. Typhon shouted out, "Don't stand there. Get her."

Una didn't look back. She knew where to go—to the stables. She ran inside, then to the back near the hayloft, and pulled on a corner manger. She pressed one side, tripping a lever, and the manger wheeled outward exposing a small hole in the stable floor. Una scrambled into the hole and pulled the manger back into its original position over her head. When she heard the click of the lever's connection, she dropped to a passageway running below the stable. Groping around in the dark, she located a nook holding wood shavings, a candle, flint, and steel.

She lit the candle and made her way into the recesses of the castle. Along the way, she found an old torch, lit it, and pushed her way through the damp stone passageway toward a room she knew was ahead.

Breaking through the spiderwebs, her voice echoed off the walls, "Your kind catch and eat flies for food. I'm going to catch and kill a venomous rat."

*****

That evening, Redcrosse and Arnax poled a raft across to the large rock formation. Climbing up to the rim, Arnax said, "See that pool in enclosure of flat rocks? There's an entrance just below the surface."

They ducked underwater into a hollow grotto that narrowed to a vent hole covered by an old iron grate. They pried the grate open to reveal a small vent hole.

"I can crawl through here and open the escape door above," Arnax said. "Meet me there."

With his sword on his back, Redcrosse swam to the edge of the rocky ridge where the escape door was hidden in the castle above the moat. He heard the bolts thrown back and Arnax stuck his head out of the open door.

"There are stairs into the cellar this way," he whispered. "Arglwydd Larn and the others are there."

Silently, carefully, and quickly, they moved through the dark passageways. Coming around a corner into a lighted area, Arnax stepped into the light.

A voice called out, "Stand!"

Redcrosse fell back into the shadows.

"It's only me, Arnax."

The guard came forward, his javelin pointed at the dwarf. "Who passes?" he said.

Redcrosse saw the renegade with the beard tied under his chin. He glared in the dim light at Arnax. "Wait!" the man said. "You're with them."

Thrusting the weapon at Arnax, he opened his mouth to shout, "Ala ..."

Redcrosse stepped out and cut the man down. He fell with a moan and a clatter. Redcrosse and Arnax froze and listened. They heard a commotion above, but no one came. Redcrosse picked up the fallen javelin. "Lead on," he said to Arnax.

Moving through the underground passageway, they came to the large cellar area that formed the dungeon. Redcrosse saw Brenin Wylle's retainers locked in the enclosures behind heavy bars. Two guards outside the door kept their attention fixed on the noise coming from the head of the stairs. Redcrosse recognized them as more of the renegades. The blond-haired man now had a steel helmet clamped down on his head. The other still wore the old, leather head guard. They both carried halberds. Someone inside the enclosures said something. The blond-haired man jabbed at him between the cell bars.

"Quiet!" he yelled.

"We'll take care of all of you soon enough," said the other.

"Why not now?"

Both guards spun around at the voice. The renegade wearing the old, leather head guard stabbed at Redcrosse with his halberd. Turning the thrust aside, Redcrosse shoved him against the enclosure. The men inside grabbed him through the bars, seizing his hands and covering his mouth. The blond-haired man shouted, "Alarm!" and slashed at Redcrosse with the blade of his halberd. Redcrosse stepped aside and thrust the retrieved javelin through the man, who fell forward with a groan. Redcrosse jumped over him to the cell door, cut through the lock bolt of the enclosure with one stroke of his sword, and jerked the door open.

Rushing out with a cry, Larn and the six men pushed the remaining renegade into the cell, took his weapon, and tied him to the cell door. Redcrosse handed the javelin to Arglwydd Larn. The craggy veteran said, "We're half-armed and outnumbered; I pity them!"

The men shouted their approval, scooped the guards' halberds, and scrambled up the stairs into the keep. At the top, a mercenary stepped inside the door and cried, "Prisoners loose!"

The mercenary brought up his bow and shot an arrow, hitting one man in the leg. Redcrosse slung *Arety* in a spinning arc and pinned the mercenary to the door. Larn and the other men ran up the narrow stairs and pushed the door open.

Larn pulled the sword from the body and tossed it back to Redcrosse.

Three more mercenaries outside the door fell to the attack of Brenin Wylle's guards. Armed with the mercenaries' weapons, Larn's men flew into the main hall of the keep. Abandoning their places at the windows, the mercenaries met their attack.

The mercenaries fought hard. Redcrosse and Larn at the head of their men, cut, parried, and thrust. Falling back, the mercenaries cried out for the rest of their fellows. Redcrosse saw more mercenaries coming down from the tower walls.

"Arnax!" he cried out. "Open the doors and lower the drawbridge."

The little man scampered among the fighting and fallen bodies, dodging blows, and disappeared into the front alcove.

*****

Coming to a room at the end of one of the passageways, Una opened the creaky door. She jammed the torch into a crack in the wall and, seeing a chair, plopped down on it. She was exhausted and her throat hurt from the pressure of Archimago's staff. Her thoughts spun in her head. She leaned back, closed her eyes, and drifted off to sleep.

Her eyes snapped open. She shook herself, stretched, and rubbed her face. She needed a weapon. The room contained some old furnishings, rolled-up faded carpets, pottery and—some old brass candleholders. Una picked up the biggest one. The weight felt good in her hand. She swung it around her head, brought it crashing down on one of the chipped terracotta pitchers, smashing it into shards.

She spoke to the walls, "I'm coming for you, Archimago."

She made her way up a set of stairs in the walled passageway, knowing there were entrances into several rooms along this level. She stopped at one with a wooden doorway and put her ear to the panels. She heard noise, commotion, and voices. Una heard one say, "There's a fight going on. The people must have broken in."

Further down the passageway was one of the main bedrooms. She would make her stand there.

Coming into the doorway, she hauled on the chain that raised the door. She could hear the noise from the fighting below. Raising the door, she saw Archimago with Typhon talking to a woman with her back to Una.

Raising the candlestick holder over her head, Una rushed toward the three people standing at the open doorway and cried, "You won't get away this time!"

Archimago, seeing the charging Una, shoved the woman into her and took off running with Typhon close behind him.

The woman crashed into Una, knocking them both to the floor. Una cringed when she saw the woman's face. She had deep, dark, demonic eyes and long fang-like teeth behind sneering, yellowed lips.

"Twit!" the woman screamed. "You prevented my getting away. You will die for that!"

She grabbed at Una, but Una pushed her back with a thrust of her legs. Una rolled over and reached for the candleholder. The older woman recovered and kicked it out of reach. Pulling a dagger from her belt, she sprang at Una.

*****

Redcrosse grabbed one of the mercenaries, slammed him against the wall, and held *Arety* to his throat.

"Where's Princess Una?" he said.

"She escaped," the man said.

"Where?"

"Who knows. Somewhere in the castle."

"Where's Archimago?"

The frightened man pointed to the stairs leading to the upper chamber. Tossing him aside, Redcrosse plunged into the throng of fighting men, flaying, and knocking them back. He fought his way to the staircase. Confronted by one man on the stairs blocking his way with a broad-blade spear, Redcrosse recognized the bald, thin man from the band of renegades.

"You!" the thin man cried out.

"Stand aside or die!" Redcrosse shouted.

The thin man leapt and thrust the spear, the blade cutting across Redcrosse's side. He turned the attack aside. The thin man regained his balance, thrust again, and caught Redcrosse in the chest with the point. The renegade shoved the spear. It stopped short. Redcrosse seized the spear blade, pulled it out, shoved it aside, and with a clean stroke of *Arety,* he cut the thin man down and climbed past the tumbling body to the upper chamber.

The hall led to two doors at either end. Redcrosse heard a noise coming from one and kicked the door in. There he saw two Unas struggling at the end of the room. One holding a dagger looked over at him and cried out, "Help me!"

In a shiny brass mirror hung on the wall across the room. Redcrosse caught sight of the reflections of the two struggling women. It was Duessa who had called out. When he looked back at her, the image of Una faded.

Duessa hissed, "So! No matter ..."

Duessa jerked her hand free and raised the dagger. Redcrosse sprang forward. Una seized Duessa's hand, pulling her to her own body. They fell to the floor. There was a loud groan, followed by a gasp. Redcrosse pulled Duessa aside. Una was spotted with blood.

"Una!"

"I'm all right," she said.

Duessa's hand still held the dagger. In their fall, Una had plunged it into her breast with a twist of her hand. Wide-eyed, Duessa looked up at Redcrosse, muttered, choked, and died.

Redcrosse held Una close for a moment. There was a new ring to the shouts from the fighting below.

"Where's Archimago?" Redcrosse said.

"He shoved that creature, Duessa, into me and took off with the monk when the fighting started. They must have gone to the outer escape door."

"Show me."

Arnax came running in. Seeing the blood on Una, he called out, "Highness, you're wounded!"

"Show Redcrosse to the outer escape door," she said.

"Follow me!" Arnax said.

They rushed down the narrow stairs. Below, the surviving mercenaries were handing their arms over to Brenin Wylle and Arglwydd Larn. Redcrosse followed the dwarf down a long hall off the keep that ended at a tapestry covering the wall. Pushing it aside, Arnax probed the stones, moved one. The wall slid back, revealing a dark passageway.

"This leads to the other escape door," the dwarf said.

Ignoring the sounds of scurrying, squeaking rats underfoot, they ran down the dark, narrow hall, keeping their balance by holding onto the walls on either side. Coming to a sharp turn, they saw a light at the end of the long passageway.

"There's the door!" Arnax cried out.

The door was unlocked. No sign of Archimago or the monk. The escape door opened onto flat ground directly under the castle's wall. The edge of the landing dropped straight off into the river.

"Is there another way in or out of the tower?" Redcrosse said.

"No. Only the drawbridge and the door where we came in at the moat on the other side of the castle."

"They must have gone out that way. Can we get there from here?"

"My mother told me never to play on the rocks around the castle's edge—but I know how to get to the other side."

# 20.

# REDCROSSE

## The Castle's Moat

ARNAX, SLIPPED SUREFOOTED over the slippery and unstable rocks forming the base of the castle. Redcrosse slipped and slid with every step. At the castle's edge, Arnax stopped, looked, and motioned for Redcrosse to come forward.

"There's the rock over the other escape door," he said.

Moving around the steep rocky ledge of the corner, Redcrosse spotted a boat emerging from the tunnel with Typhon rowing in strong strokes and Archimago, still in bishop's robes, urging him on.

"They're getting away," Arnax cried out.

"We'll have to swim after them," Redcrosse said.

Arnax stopped, eyes wide, and sucked in his breath.

"What is it?" Redcrosse said.

"I can't swim."

"Get on my back and hold on."

Redcrosse climbed down to the river's edge.

"What if I slip?" Arnax said.

"You'd better not."

Handing Arnax his sword, Redcrosse helped the little man climb on his back. Seeing the pair in the boat had outdistanced them, Redcrosse struck out for the other bank. Arnax gripped Redcrosse's neck with one arm and clutched the sword in the other. Redcrosse struggled in the long swim, his wounds and the strain of fighting taking their toll on him. Reaching the shore, he climbed onto the rocks and collapsed, trying to catch his breath.

Arnax called out, "Hurry! They've got a wagon."

Redcrosse spoke in short gasps, "Run ... the square ... my horse."

Arnax took off, his short legs carrying him in the direction of the square. Redcrosse crawled up the bank and watched as Archimago and Typhon sped off down the road in the wagon headed for the border.

He tried to get to his feet but fell to his knees on the bank in a fit of exhaustion.

Everything spun around. He closed his eyes.


"Sir Redcrosse."

Redcrosse awoke. Arnax leaned over him holding the reins of the big gray. The knight labored to his feet, grabbed the stirrup, and pulled himself onto Telum, then reached down and pulled the little man up behind him.

"Take that way," Arnax said. "The road they took takes a long time to get to the border. We can go faster through the hills."

Redcrosse, with Arnax at his back, took off toward the high hill. After climbing it and coming down a narrow trail on the other side, Redcrosse saw the trail had become just a dirt path between the hills that came out into a draw. There, it forked in two opposite directions. Arnax pointed the way and the big warhorse took the path in long, quick strides.

The path ran along the foot of a high, steep hill. Its brown, sheer slopes rose into a dome-shape with two large gullies on either side. This gave the hill the appearance of a huge gnome face staring down at them.

"Around this hill!" Arnax called out. "We'll meet the main road."

The path curved along a rise of one of the lower slopes along the side of the hill. The big gray surged and pulled his way up the hill where the path leveled off. At its crest, Redcrosse saw the ribbon of the main road. Scanning down the road, he saw dust rising in a draw.

He spurred the big gray down the side of the hill and galloped over an abandoned farm field to the main road.

"There's an old bridge over that wash," Arnax said. "We can stop them there."

Redcrosse saw the bridge spanned a dry gully and was supported by two rickety timber braces. A few yards away, a large boulder sat on a rise overlooking the draw of the dry gully. He rode up to it, dismounted, and dug the soft ground from under the large rock.

"Come, Arnax," he called out.

They both leaned against the boulder and pushed. With a groaning sound, the huge stone moved, rolled down the rise, picked up momentum and struck one of the old supports under the bridge. A large crack sounded. The old bridge broke loose from its moorings and leaned to one side. Redcrosse took up a position behind some trees and Arnax crawled into the nearby bushes.

Typhon lashed hard with the reins at the horse pulling the wagon. Coming over the rise in the road to the bridge, Archimago looked up ahead.

Seeing the tilted, broken bridge, he called out "Typhon! The bridge ... Stop!"

The big man jerked back on the reins and pulled the horse to a stop before the leaning bridge. Arnax darted out from the underbrush and jammed a long piece of wood behind the wheel. Grabbing a long handled trident from the wagon, the large monk jumped out and chased after the dwarf. The dwarf ran past Redcrosse who rode out to confront the hooded man in the robe.

"Stand!" the knight called out.

The big monk raised his trident. Redcrosse held the sword in front of him.

"Go on, Typhon," he said. "I only want the Wizard."

Typhon gave a roar and charged the horse with the trident. Redcrosse turned aside the thrust with a swinging parry, spurred Telum, and drove the charger into the big man, knocking him to the ground. The cowl fell back from his head. When he rolled back to his feet, Redcrosse jerked his sword in shock.

One piercing eye shone out of the middle of Typhon's

forehead. His mouth drawn back in a growling snarl showed snaggled, sharp teeth. He grabbed up the fallen trident.

"He's a Cyclops!" Arnax cried out.

Running up from the other side of the wagon, Archimago swung his bishop's crook at Redcrosse. Redcrosse shifted the rump of the big gray horse in a swinging cross block and knocked Archimago from his feet. Arnax dashed up and struck Archimago over the shoulder with a thick stick. It shattered, doing little harm. Archimago rose and cracked the dwarf across the head with the crook. The little man fell and lay still.

Typhon jumped up and pulled Redcrosse from Telum's back and sent the knight rolling across the ground. He stabbed at Redcrosse with the trident. The three needle-sharp points of the blades struck the ground. Redcrosse rolled to one side, came up on one knee, and cut at Typhon.

Typhon blocked it and jabbed again. Archimago came up and moved in, getting Redcrosse between him and Typhon. Redcrosse feinted to Typhon's head and spun, striking at Archimago. The Wizard caught the sword on the ornate metal end of the crook. Redcrosse dashed from between them, back toward his horse. The two rushed him, Typhon thrusting and Archimago swinging. Redcrosse jumped to one side and shoved the Wizard into the Cyclops.

Typhon shoved Archimago away and jabbed at Redcrosse with the trident. One of the three blades pierced Redcrosse's left shoulder. He grabbed the weapon at its axis with his left hand and thrust *Arety* into the body of the Cyclops with his right.

The single eye opened wide, the red mouth popped open. Typhon uttered a choked sound, let go of the trident, and fell to the ground. Redcrosse tore the trident from his shoulder, jerked *Arety* from Typhon's body, and spun around to face Archimago.

The Wizard stared for an instant at the body of Typhon. He stepped back, grabbed the crook, and twisted it. A click. He whipped out a long sword blade from inside the staff. Tossing the staff aside, Archimago attacked Redcrosse with a two-handed cut to his head.

Putting the shoulder pain out of his mind, Redcrosse parried, fixing his attention on the man in front of him. The Wizard thrust and countered with great skill. Redcrosse parried his thrust.

"You fight well, Wizard," he said.

"Dog! I cut men's heads while you still pissed your pants."

He attacked Redcrosse again and again. The fury of his blows drove Redcrosse back. Archimago slashed Redcrosse across the wounded shoulder. Redcrosse flinched, shook off the searing pain.

Seeing his advantage, Archimago renewed his attack to that side. Redcrosse was growing weaker and slower countering the fierce blows. After a thrust with the cane sword at Redcrosse's wounded side again, Archimago retreated to make a step-in cut. Redcrosse brought *Arety* up from his toes in a wide arc and with a shout, cut at Archimago's head. The

Wizard raised his hand and parried. *Arety* broke the blade of the cane sword in two pieces. Archimago stood with Redcrosse's sword pushing on his Adam's apple.

"I'm unarmed. I yield," he said.

Redcrosse did not waver and kept the weapon at Archimago's throat.

"You'll be tried for all your crimes," he said.

Archimago's large round eyes were even wider now.

"Spare me," he pleaded.

Still pressing the sword to his throat, Redcrosse moved Archimago toward the wagon. He looked over and saw the still form of Arnax on the ground and froze.

In that instant, Archimago pushed aside the sword point, dashed over, grabbed up the fallen trident, swung the sharp weapon hard, wheeled around and thrust it into the face of his opponent. Redcrosse stepped in past the trident's triple blades and in one stroke cut off Archimago's head.

The wall eyes expressed surprise. Lips moved in a noiseless scream. The severed head fell from the collapsing body.

The knight ran to the fallen dwarf. When he picked up the little man, Arnax gave a groan, "My head ..." he said.

"You're fine."

The dwarf managed a weak smile, "Thank you."


Redcrosse and Arnax loaded Archimago's and Typhon's remains into the wagon. They drove back to the place where the highway forked into two directions and buried them at dusk in a common grave at the crossroads, leaving behind no trace or marker.

When they arrived back at the castle, the people were dancing and singing in the streets. Brenin Wylle and Una, surrounded by their subjects, met Redcrosse and Arnax in the square in front of the tower. Arglwydd Larn helped Redcrosse down from the wagon, took him where he could wash his wounds and gave him his tabard.

Arnax gave everyone a vivid report of Archimago's end. Brenin Wylle embraced Redcrosse as the people cheered. Una stood at her father's side. The veil was gone. Her smile radiant. Her eyes fixed on the man in front of her.

"My name is George," he told them. "My father was a Saxon king. I'm still bound to my Queene's service."

Looking first at Una, he turned to Brenin Wylle.

"But when I return," he said. "I will seek your permission for the hand of Princess Una to be my wife—if she will have me."

His smile now grown wide, Brenin Wylle turned, looking at his daughter Una. She looked into her father's face, then looked back at the knight in front of her.

"I will," she said.

# 21.

# SAINT GEORGE

## Troynouvaux

THE GATES TO TROYNOUVAUX were open wide. The Redcrosse Knight rode in on his warhorse Telum. Cheering people lined the way to the Queene's palace. The sounds of drums, flutes, bagpipes, and harps filled the air. Little girls handed him garlands of flowers. Little boys shouted and waved. The noise made Telum skittish as the big gray danced along the cobblestoned street.

At the palace gates, the guards raised their weapons in salute. When Redcrosse dismounted in the courtyard, Thobus, a grin on his horse-face, took the reins and led Telum to the sables.

His fellow knights rushed forward. Sir Allyne embraced him.

"Young rogue," he said. "You've done well."

Redcrosse started to remove his sword belt. Sir Allyne shook his head and stopped his hand.

"Nay," he said. "*Arety* is yours. It always was."

The list master embraced Redcrosse once more while his fellows greeted him and slapped him on the back. Sir

Allyne growled at them, "Care. Can you not see he's been wounded?"

Sir Uther Pendragon embraced his friend.

"Only scratches," he said.

Redcrosse moved to take off the Gold Dragon's Head medallion.

"Your family crest saved me twice, Sir Uther," he said.

"Keep it always as a symbol of the bond between our two houses."

Redcrosse looked over at a short, dark, stocky man, his face in a grin, wearing the bright blue tabard of a new knight. Redcrosse embraced him and said, "Sir Barstair!"

"I'm still getting used to it. I owe apologies for my conduct on the lists that day."

"No! I owe you much for that lesson. It saved my life more than once."

Sir Allyne broke in, "Her Majesty awaits."


Outside the throne room, Minatrix glided up to Redcrosse, kissed his cheek, stepped back, and looked him over.

"Well, no longer the impish boy who used to put frogs in my sewing basket," she chimed. The tall Faerie motioned him to follow. The Queene's hawk-faced personal guards bowed a quick nod, then swung open the massive doors to the great room.

Redcrosse entered to cheers and applause from members of the court. Queene Gloriana sat on her throne on the raised dais. The court stepped back, opening a path directly to the throne. The Queene's Beadle struck the floor with his staff and announced, "The Redcrosse Knight returns from his quest."

Redcrosse crossed the floor and dropped to one knee before the Queene.

"Is the dragon defeated, Sir George?" she asked.

A hush descended on the assembled court at the investing of the new name.

Sir George said, "All the dragons are no more, Majesty."

Echoing throughout the court, his response provoked murmurs.

Queene Gloriana said, "Before the court dies of want to know, Sir George. Tell Us what you mean by 'all of the dragons.'"

"The dragon I slew by the Cave of Winds in the North Country was a noble beast. The misery it caused came from its own raw nature. But the dragons Archimago, Typhon, Duessa, and the dark brothers, Sir Sansfoy, Sir Sansjoy and Sir Sansloy, were the evil ones. I beheaded the hypocrite and liar Wizard near the border of the North Country. I destroyed all of them out of duty. The beast, I somewhat regret. The others, I do not."

"Do you still have matters there that need be resolved?"

"No, Your Majesty."

"Then, you may resume your service. Rise, Sir George, your quest is complete."

"Thank you, Your Majesty."

The Queene motioned for Minatrix to approach. Leaning

forward, they spoke in whispers in the rapid, buzzing language of the Faeries. Minatrix bowed her head and left the room.

The Queene said, "It is Our desire that you spend the remainder of the day with your fellow knights. They'll want to know all the details of your quest. At sunset, come to Lady Minatrix. She will bring you to my private chambers. We'll then discuss matters further."

The Queene rose. The Beadle struck the floor and announced that the audience was over.

In the barracks, Sir George related each part of his adventures several times. A patient storyteller, he was reserved, reluctant to give great details. His young friends devoured each word spoken and asked even more questions after each telling. Redcrosse recounted, explained, and repeated until Sir Allyne noted it was time for him to leave for his audience.

The list master and Sir Uther walked Sir George to the castle.

"And the maiden?" Sir Uther asked.

"I've asked her to be my wife."

Sir Allyne raised his eyes to look at the sky.

"The life of a knight is hard on a wife," he said. "We go off, fight, and adventure. Too often they're left home for long periods of time, having to raise the children alone and growing bitter. Always spend time with your family—even at the cost of other things. A man has no greater wealth than his family."

"You never married?" Sir George said.

"That's why I speak with such authority."

Clapping George on the back and taking his hand, Sir Allyne pulled both young men to him in a rib-cracking embrace.

"I've not lacked for sons," he said. "I've watched all of you wide-eyed pups with a thirst for the fight grow into fierce young dogs. A few times, I had to use a heavy hand."

Sir Uther shook his red head.

"You never held back in the lists," he said. "If we were being pampered, it was damn rough treatment."

"That's true," Sir George said. "More than once I went in with bruised ribs."

"You two were different," the list master said. "You've the talent of weaponry but none of the savagery that usually goes with mastering it. You fight hard, but you can let it go when it's over. I've always seen greatness in both of you."

Sir Allyne stopped, wiped his eyes.

"Enough," he said. "I'm getting too sentimental. It's time to leave. Farewell, you two."

Sir Allyne hugged them both once more and walked away, back straight. He didn't look back.

Uther smiled at George.

"Rogue," he said. "You've outdone us all."

"None could have happened without all your help."

"And now, a lady awaits you."

"Yes. And she knows her own mind."

"She'll have to. You're much in need of teaching."

"I'll learn."

"I'll go now, George. I wish you well in everything."

"Duty calls us, Uther. I thank you for your friendship."

Sir Uther embraced his friend for the last time.

"Go," he said. "Your destiny awaits."

Redcrosse went inside where the tall Faerie waited. She led him up the stairs by a back passageway to the Queene's private apartments. A hawk-faced guard opened the door for her.

Queene Gloriana sat inside, gazing out of the window. She acknowledged Sir George's bow without rising.

"Come here, Sir George."

He came and stood beside her.

"I have another task for you," she said.

"Majesty?"

"Return to the North Country and marry Princess Una. While danger from Archimago and Duessa is no more, the world is still full of those who lust for power. The Kingdom of the North Country is still vulnerable to scoundrels and rogues and needs your assistance."

She turned her dark eyes to look in his eyes.

"I want you to leave immediately," she said.

"Majesty."

Sir George backed to the door, bowed, and left.

\*\*\*\*\*

*"There, over the plain, rides Sir George, the Redcrosse knight," the hermit said.*

Queene Gloriana sat looking out of the window without moving. The door to her chamber opened. Minatrix and the hermit came in.

Queene Gloriana did not look up.

"He's going," she said.

Minatrix nodded.

"It's time," the hermit said.

For several moments they exchanged no words but looked out at the lone figure of Redcrosse on the back of the big gray warhorse riding out toward the North Country. The dying day drenched dark, golden hues over the grasslands and fields, its glint turning the white of Redcrosse's tabard into a sheet of shining gold, the cross on his back reddened even more in the fiery sunset.

"He has but an inkling of his destiny," Minatrix said.

"Yes," the Queene said. "But he'll learn."

"There, over the plain, rides Sir George, the Redcrosse knight," the hermit said. "Future Saint George and patron protector of England."

www.ingramcontent.com/pod-product-compliance
Lightning Source LLC
Chambersburg PA
CBHW070549100726
47907CB00004B/1325